PERFECTLY FORMED

SHORT STORIES

AVA MING   ROSANNE DINGLI   SUE BRENNAN

CAROLINE JAMES MACKIE   STEVE WADE   LUKE VARNEY

KATE WRITER   LAUREN WORDSWORTH   KATHRYN T

Junoberry
Books

CONTENTS

INTRODUCTION

Welcome to our *Perfectly Formed* Anthology, a collection of stories from our first annual short story competition. This was was launched in October 2023 and we were lucky enough to receive a huge number of creative stories.

This published anthology collection includes the competition winner, runners-up and the other entries that made the shortlist for this competition.

We have a wide variety of shorts in here, from stories about loss and the difficult nature of families, to ones about instant attraction and lust. We have intriguing mysteries, interesting adventures and journeys and some darker tales about death, murder and abuse. There is definitely something in here for all tastes and we hope we have selected a wide range of styles and voices to keep you engaged and interested throughout.

We are sure that these writers will continue to produce high quality stories - make sure you keep an eye out for your favourites in the future and support what else they have to offer.

We hope you enjoy the stories as much as we did.

Junoberry Books

INTRODUCTION

THE WINNERS AND RUNNERS-UP

Here are the winners and runners-up for our Perfectly Formed 2023 short story competition.

All of these stories and the other shortlisted ones can be found within this collection.

WINNER:

Addicted by Ava Ming

RUNNERS-UP:

Midnight on the Water by Rosanne Dingli

Two Funerals by Sue Brennan

SHORTLISTED STORIES:

Disownment by Caroline James Mackie

Blood Brother by Steve Wade

The Devil's Resting Place by Luke Varney

The Incident at Sea by Kate Mahony

The Secrets within Hartwick Manor by Lauren Wordsworth

Dirty Laundry by Ava Ming

Giving Death the Slip by Kathryn T

All of the entries were read and recommended anonymously, and this led to two stories being selected by one writer, Ava Ming (one of which was our winner). We contemplated only putting one of these stories forward but wanted to honour the process we had put in place and therefore decided to include both.

WINNER:
ADDICTED BY AVA MING

ADDICTED

BY AVA MING

I NEVER MEANT TO STEAL FROM MY MAN, BUT ONCE I'D DONE IT A few times I couldn't stop. Not my fault. I was addicted, apparently.

I got pretty sick a while ago, a depressive illness my doctor said. It's weird 'cos you ain't got no obvious signs, but inside you're not yourself and it's just too hard to deal with ordinary stuff like work, shopping and bills and everything. It's like having to push your whole body, arms aloft, chin high, through thick mud in slow motion. That's probably the best way to describe it.

The psychiatrist fingered his side part and adjusted his pert, navy blue bow tie. He drew me straight lines connected by little round dots, drawing upside down so it was facing me, then he leaned back in his leather chesterfield armchair all smug and with his fingers steepled, like he'd created a master-piece from a museum.

'You see, Nicole, with most people, these lines, which represent a liquid called a neuro-transmitter, go from point to point but with a mental health problem like yours, there's a short-fall, see?' He tapped his pencil against the paper.

'What's a neuron-transporter?' The pleather chair stuck to my skin making me fidgety. My eyes flickered over the certificates on the wall behind his head, the print too small to read on most of 'em. The room smelt of furniture polish, but dust still clung to the plastic yellow daffodils in the window.

'Here.' He drew over the lines, making them thicker and darker, repeating that the lack of this liquid was why I felt so miserable all the time.

'You also have an addictive personality. Was there anything you particularly liked to do when you were a little girl?'

I fiddled with my earring, pulled a face. 'Like wha'?'

'Ball games? Knitting? Skipping?'

'I liked reading comics.'

'That's normal, but often in childhood there's some indication of these future addictions.'

'I don't do drugs! You think just because I'm black that...' I shut-up when he picked up his pen and opened my folder. Didn't want him to add *chip on the shoulder,* to my diagnosis.

'I mean,' he scribbled something briefly and shut my file. 'When some people find something pleasurable, the brain latches on to it and they can spend hours repeating it or wanting to do it every chance they get, hardly even realizing what's going on. It helps them to forget about the real world.'

'It don't apply to me. Anyway, what's wrong with doing stuff over and over again, especially if you ain't hurting nobody?'

'Addictive behaviour can stop you from progressing.'

He droned on, I zoned out until he said he was signing me off from my job so I'd have space to gather my thoughts. I worked as a picker-packer in a warehouse. Same thing five days a week from eight-thirty to four, with a half hour lunch.

I swiped my prescription for anti-depressants off his desk and left. Why were doctors never happy unless they stuck a label on you and told you how to behave? How did he know I had thoughts I wanted gathering, how come that wasn't addictive?

The stupid pills the quack gave me slowed me right down. I did try to keep going and still have a life even if I didn't have a job. I met the girls for a boogie and a pint on Saturday nights, but I couldn't drink while I was on meds so partying soon got boring and once my money ran out, I stopped going.

Six weeks after I'd been signed off, my manager wrote if I didn't come back the following Monday they'd assume I'd resigned. I was too doped up to argue. It was easier to ignore their bullying, so I let them fire me.

Wasn't long before my phone rang less, my TV was on 24/7 and my curtains barely opened, just like my front door. Half the time I forgot what day it was. To fight off the lethargy which kept me glued to the settee, I'd occasionally go down the high street, buy a magazine and see how the world was managing without me. I'd pick up fags, a bottle of milk, cans of coke, some chocolates, bread, sarnie stuff, a tin or two of baked beans and a couple packets of biscuits.

I was in limbo waiting for my addictive patterns to surface so I could work out what the hell the Doc was on about, but nothing happened. I didn't develop an obsessive/compulsive need to wash my hands, switch the lights on and off, or pat my head thirty times before I went to bed. I didn't obsess over wool ply and knitting patterns. I didn't develop any new habits or re-discover any annoying childhood traits. I figured he must have plucked the diagnosis out of thin air. Addictive personality my arse!

'Mom?' I called out like I always did when I came in from playing but she didn't answer. I rushed into the living room expecting her to be watching TV but there was a man there wearing a loose, half-buttoned shirt with a big round hairy tummy hanging over his dirty jeans. His hair flopped between his eyes and he smiled with yellow teeth while horses raced across the TV screen in front of him.

'Hello little girl. You been out playing?'

'Where's my mommy?' I blinked a lot 'cos I was all confused. My mom wasn't where I'd left her and this man was in our house, sitting on our couch like it was no big deal.

'Shop. She'll be back in a minute. It's Nicole isn't it? Your mom said you can stop with me. Want a biscuit?' He shook half a packet of Custard Creams at me.

'Nah.'

He leaned forward and I backed off without even realising how close I'd got to him. I'd planned to run in and flop on the couch next to mom like usual, but he'd stopped me in my tracks.

I tried to back off some more but he grabbed my arm, making me stand still.

'When's my mom coming back?' I asked him, when what I really wanted to say was when are you going away?'

'Soon, soon.' He'd said, flashing those big teeth at me like the wolf in Little Red Riding Hood. As if he'd never learnt how to smile properly.

'I'm going back out to play.' I wriggled my arm out of his grasp and he let me go.

'It's okay, I'm her friend, I've known her for ages. You too, when you were a little 'un, still in your pram. You won't remember me, but that's all right.'

I stared at him, trying to think if I had seen him before, but my mind was blank. He said he was my mom's friend, maybe, he was okay?

'Come here a bit, let's have a look at ya.' He pulled me onto his lap, played with the ribbon in my hair and tried to cuddle me but I was stiff and awkward in his arms. I tried to get down and sit on the couch a little bit away from him but he didn't seem to want me to go.

'I'm your Uncle Joe. You 'member me, don't you?' He said again.

I shook my head.

'Your mom told me to watch ya, said you'd be as good as gold. You're gonna be good for me aren't ya?'

His breath bounced off my cheek. It smelt funny, like a mixture of cigarettes and beer. His face was so close to mine it felt like he was giving me something I shouldn't have, something personal which should have been for a grown woman like my mom. He'd said he was my Uncle Joe but I didn't know him and I didn't want to.

'Cute little thing aren't ya?' He stroked my cheek and I squirmed trying to shake him off.

'Wanna watch TV with me?'

'No, I've gotta wee.'

Uncle Joe held my hand and walked me to the bathroom, like I was the visitor and he lived at ours.

'I can go by myself.' I tried to yank my hand away, but he held it tight.

'Course you can, you're a clever seven-year-old. I bet you can do lots of things by yourself.'

'I'm nine actually. Mom says I'm only little bit.'

'Small, but perfectly formed.'

In the bathroom he knelt down so he was the same height as me, touched my face and ran his thick, rough fingertips over my eyelids, my cheeks and my chin, onto my neck and my shoulders and further down till he'd felt all over my body. He kept on talking but I don't remember much. He stayed there watching me pee even though I'd told him to go outside. His flies were undone and a pink shiny thing poked out the top of his pants.

When mom came back I wasn't in my bedroom and Joe wasn't on the settee watching Saturday afternoon racing. We were still in the bathroom and I was naked, my t-shirt and shorts in Uncle Joe's hands and the bathroom door locked.

Mom battered at the door with her fists when she heard me crying, screaming out my name and swearing at Uncle Joe till he undid the lock.

She stared in horror at the bloody streaks on the inside of my legs and tried to punch him in the face but he dodged the blow. She shouted she was gonna call the cops but Uncle Joe grabbed her by her hair, twisting her neck and telling her to think twice about that, then he slapped her a good one before running out of our back door and up through our garden to the back alley that went down to the train tracks.

Later when the police came, I learnt two strange new words: Rape. Testify. No-one explained what they meant. A few weeks after, we moved 'cos someone slashed our car tyres and my mom was knocked out cold in our living room when a brick thrown through our window hit her on the head.

A police lady asked us if we thought Uncle Joe's brother, Guy, had thrown the brick. She gave me a book with pictures of bears on the covers and smooth white pages inside. She told me it was called a diary and that I should put all of my thoughts in it whenever they were too much to hold in my head, especially if I didn't want to tell anybody. But instead, I wrote down more new words which I'd heard the coppers saying: Witness Intimidation. Court Date.

I used the dictionary to make sure I got the right spellings and I kept on adding to the list, page after page after page till the book got full and I had to get a new one, so I could start making lists all over again.

After that I had a different mom. She was still in my mom's body, she still wore my mom's clothes, but she never laughed any more or made herself look pretty or even took me to the park. She just smoked, drank whisky and always wanted to know where I was.

She never gave me any more Uncles and we had so many different homes I got used to being the new girl at school, the new girl on the street. The girl with the quiet mom who kept herself to herself, the girl who knew words no-one else her age knew. The girl who liked to stay in her room and write things down instead of going outside to play.

When I heard my mom chucking up behind the locked bathroom door every night after dinner, I wrote down Bulimia Nervosa. Agoraphobia: when she stopped going outside. Unemployed: when she lost her job 'cos of too many days on the sick. Vagrant: when the council took back our house and made us homeless 'cos we hadn't kept up with the rent. Orphaned: when my mom died when I was fourteen. Conform: when I was in foster care and they locked me in isolation for scrapping with the other kids and sending one to hospital.

Free: when they gave me my own flat at sixteen. Whore: after my umpteenth one-night stand when I got the clap after searching for love in all the wrong men. Stupid: when I couldn't enrol in beauty school where I'd planned to spend all day messing about with lotions and potions, hoping to feel good about myself by making other women feel good about themselves.

I wanted to work on a big cruise ship like I'd seen on TV. I imagined pampering rich clients who would reward me with big tips as we sailed through the Mediterranean, the Caribbean, Alaska and the Panama bowl or basin or bucket, whatever they called it.

I'd have done that for years till it was all a blur, saved my money and gone to live in whichever country I'd liked the best. But the college wouldn't accept me 'cos I needed better grades in my school exams. Better grades to slap cold cream onto old ladies' cellulite and bingo wings.

My lists were all I had to stop me thinking about the day when my mom went to get fish and chips for tea and left me with a strange man who made me wee in front of him and ruined our lives forever.

I fumbled for a cigarette in the pack on the floor by the settee but it was empty. I snuggled down for a nap, but the sofa reeked of nicotine making me want one even more. I dragged myself up, threw on a jumper over my tatty t-shirt and jogging bottoms, tied my hair in a messy top-knot, shuffled into my flip-flops and trundled around the corner onto the high street and into Zak's mini-mart. If the shop was quiet Zak might split a pack and let me have some loose fags for a couple of quid, but there was a long queue at the till and Zak was nowhere to be seen. Just my luck. I hovered near the counter hoping he'd appear and sort me out quick.

A stranger's stare sent prickles down the back of my neck, like someone rubbing an ice-lolly against my skin. I turned to face him, cuss words at the ready. He was a bit too close for comfort and a foot taller than me.

'I think you dropped this.'

He handed me a familiar looking bank card, but I'd left mine at home. I pulled it closer pretending to check the name, suddenly wishing I'd done something with my hair and worn better clothes. The man held onto it, his fingers inching forward until he was holding my hand. Cheeky bugger.

'Do I know you?' I asked him, trying to be all flirty.

'Not yet.'

I'd spent so much time staring at the TV instead of being around normal people I thought his average smile was gorgeous. I clocked his basket while I waited to see what he was gonna do next. There were no family sized bags, tins or boxes and his ring finger was empty with no trace of a shadow.

'Brian.' He shook my hand stroking my palm with his thumb.

'Nicky.'

I should have pulled away but it had been ages since I'd touched another human being, let alone a half-decent bloke. Plus I liked the casual way he wore his polo shirt with the collar up and the not-too-tight fit of his jeans.

We queued together and he laughed at my weak jokes the way men always do when they wanna sleep with you. He bought me a full pack of 20 cigarettes and offered me a lift but I told him I don't get into cars with strangers so he walked me home instead.

After that things get a little foggy, like I can only remember the outline and not the detail. I think he came in and pulled a face at the mess of clothes and dirty plates and the sloppy pile of newspapers, magazines and junk mail. Did he cook me dinner from his own shopping; tuna, and spring onions, maybe potatoes? I might have said I didn't eat onions and he might have said I'd eat his. I'm pretty sure he stayed the night, used a condom then called me the next day.

'We met for a reason,' he said when I answered the phone, smiling at the vague memory of his brown eyes, his short-ish haircut and his thin but nicely shaped lips. He suggested I increase the dosage of my anti-depressants, thought it might help me get better quicker. Seemed like a good idea, so, without telling the quack, I did.

Six weeks later I was living in his smartly done-up, disinfectant-smelling semi, down the better end of our district, kissing him goodbye when he went off to his supervisor's job at some office, never asked where, didn't care, and dishing up his dinner when he came home.

Brian thinks I've given my place back to the council but I haven't. I may be on pills and living in a fog and it might seem like Brian's taking over, but he's not.

'Nicole! You seen my purse?' Mom's footsteps tapped along the hallway lino.

I sat on the red vinyl settee in our lounge, its knitted cushions rubbing against my thighs. A purse crammed full of banknotes lay hot underneath my bum. I was eleven years old.

'Nicole Kemeisha Thompson!' She forced all three of my names through tired lips. At the front door she searched through coat pockets, placed up high on plastic wall hooks.

'Child! You deaf?'

'Coming!' I grabbed a handful of notes, stuffed them down my jeans, pushed the rest back into her purse and threw it onto the sideboard.

'Yes mom?' My eyes were wide, my shoulders hunched, my palms turned upwards just like her whenever she had the rent man, or the gas man, or the bailiff standing in front of her.

She tutted, strode into the lounge and spotted her purse. Her starched blue, cleaner's uniform scrapped against my skin as she pushed past me.

'I'm late.' She grabbed her coat and wrenched open the front door. 'Back around nine. Sandwiches in the kitchen if you get hungry.' She kissed my forehead. 'Make sure you lock the door behind me. Do it right now and don't open the door for no-one except your Aunty Eunice, she'll be here in an hour.'

She'd gone, without once looking into my eyes. I pulled a face, mouthed the words "Lock the door behind me," while I did as I'd been told. I took the money out of my clothes, went up to my room, closed the curtains, opened a drawer and retrieved a shoe box decorated with glitter and multi-coloured stars.

I tucked my knees underneath me on the thin carpet and smoothed out the new notes, counting fivers, tens and twenty's, stopping when I got to a total of £55. I took out my special pen, the one with purple ink, opened my latest diary and wrote down another new word, using my dictionary to check the spelling: Disregarded.

'Been thinking about getting a job. Maybe some domestic work, something like that.'

The news was on but Brian wasn't watching it. He was sitting on his fat arse staring into space, musing over whether to take a bath, go down the pub, or hassle me for sex which provided a release for him and did nothing for me.

'Why?' He mumbled, biting off a hangnail.

'I wanna get out of the house a bit more, maybe help out with the bills and stuff.'

'An extra tenner a week from cleaning someone's loo? We'll be rich!'

The bastard bared his teeth in a predatory smile, verbally slapping me down for having an original thought.

'I'm going upstairs,' I declared to the back of his big round head.

'Want some company?'

PERFECTLY FORMED

He fingered the small brown bottle of poppers he kept in his pocket. I hated the way he sniffed it when we were doing it, stuffing it up his nose while smirking at me, as if he was inhaling the chemicals for my benefit.

'Sort out my bath?' He called as I left the room.

Wipe your arse for you as well, shall I? He was so rubbish. Worse than a two-year-old.

I ran the bath as hot as I could without scalding him. I was growing to hate him, not that I'd ever really loved him. I suppose in the beginning he'd been my saviour but now he had me right where he wanted me. I was old news.

I shut the bathroom door and sat on the loo seat lid waiting for my tears to tell me whether to leave him or stay, but the blasted anti-depressants dulled my emotions. Keeping me on an even keel, the doctor called it. Turning me into a flipping zombie, more like.

Brian's work trousers hung on the back of the door. He always got changed in the bathroom before parading naked across the landing, showing off his pot belly and saggy butt, flinging his clothes onto the bed for me to sort and wash. I grabbed the trousers, surprised when wads of notes fell from the pockets. I locked the door and counted. There was over £400 in tens, twenties and a couple of £50 notes.

'Brian?' I bit my lip, holding back my questions. As if he'd admit to me what was going on. I was just a glorified housekeeper who gave it up for a decent roof over my head.

'Bath ready?' He called back.

'Yeah, in a minute!' I scooped the money into his trousers minus about sixty quid which I pushed into my pockets and down my bra before sneaking into the bedroom. Brian's stinky work pants had made my decision for me.

I heard him plodding upstairs. I knew any second he'd call me in for 'quality time,' watching him wrinkle like a prune while he gabbed on about his day. It never occurred to him to ask me about mine.

'Nicky, you coming or what?'

The water sloshed over the edge as he got into the bath.

'Gimme a sec!' I made a beeline for my handbags which Brian avoided, said they were too girly. I stuffed the notes inside and stashed them all in a suitcase, shoving it under the bed and trying not to smile myself silly.

From then on, I'd run his bath, shake his pants until the notes found their way into my slippers, or my knickers, or my pockets and from there into my special hiding place. I never took more than a hundred or so at a time and if Brian ever noticed he never commented.

He didn't go out more often than usual. He hadn't bought any new clothes or jewellery or changed his car. He wasn't into gambling as far as I knew apart from some work do at the greyhound races and he also never travelled so I had no idea what the money was for, let alone where he got it from. It was a total mystery.

I sorted out my rent arrears and paid off outstanding bills on my old home. Spent about five hundred quid altogether. Apart from that I was saving, 'cos when I got about two or three thousand pounds I was gonna leave. Pack a bag, hop on a flight and disappear.

I sat on top of the double bed watching the flat screen TV, comfy in my brushed cotton day-pyjamas, my hair all glossy and smelling of apple shampoo, a glass of coke with a dash of rum at my elbow. I flicked through the shopping channels and afternoon soaps clutching my stash of two and a half fabulous thousand pounds.

'Nicole?'

Brian was standing over me with an odd look on his face. I must have fallen asleep. I kept eye contact while furtively reaching for my money.

'What you doing?'

I scratched my head. 'Er, nothing.'

'Get the tea on and run me a bath, yeah?'

He left and I scrambled around searching for my dough. It wasn't on the bed and it hadn't fallen on the floor. Where the hell was it? On my hands and knees I pulled out the suitcase and unzipped it, shook my handbags one by one, stuck my fingers deep into the tightly sewn inner pockets. They were all empty, the fucker had stolen my money.

I was still on my knees when he came back, the front of his shoe touching my thigh, his eyebrows raised, his mouth open. He dropped a sheet of paper into my lap. It was a receipt from the housing department for the keys to my flat with a note thanking me for handing them in, although we both knew that I hadn't.

'Time we sorted things out, eh? No point leaving it any longer. You don't need that flat anymore. To be honest it was a bit of a surprise finding the keys, thought you'd handed them back ages ago.'

So, he'd definitely been through my stuff. I stood, folded up the receipt and tossed it onto the bed where I'd been sitting.

'Don't worry about cooking, changed my mind. I'm in the mood for a curry.'

He touched my arm before leaving the room. A one-fingered press, reminding me I'd sunk seamlessly into his world, losing myself and my dreams and he'd do whatever it took to make sure I stayed lost.

I flopped back onto the bed and closed my eyes, opened my diary in the privacy of my mind and added my final word to the bottom of my list: Trapped.

RUNNERS-UP:

MIDNIGHT ON THE WATER BY ROSANNE DINGLI & TWO FUNERALS BY SUE BRENNAN

MIDNIGHT ON THE WATER

BY ROSANNE DINGLI

HE SAW HER LEAVE A SIDE STREET, CROSS THE ROAD TO THE walkway along the shore. He'd seen her before; a shape whose skirt and hair blew lightly behind her, even if there was no wind. From where he sat on the dune with his groundsheet and small fire, she looked like a wraith, thin but hardy and bendy like a bough. The realization she was younger than he'd imagined struck him. The skin on her arms and face was apricot fresh.

It would be dark soon. He looked away from her and pushed another twig onto the flames. It crackled and flared immediately.

'I've seen you here before.' Her voice boomed; a low register, a contralto tone that filled the evening. A lyric out of a song.

She looked down at him from a distance of three yards, perhaps four, saying five clear words. Was it an introduction, or an accusation, as if he were trespassing, meant to send him away? On top of the dune, against the sky, she took on a statuesque appearance, suddenly a strong bronze figure. Voices had that power, he saw, to change one's impression of a person.

'It will be dark soon.' Five more words. A kind of curfew? A car passed on the road and turned her into a silhouette for three seconds.

He gestured to suggest she should come closer to the fire.

A voice could change one's impression of a figure, but a smile could change everything else, even atmosphere, surroundings, temperature, time. From a grey dune at the edge of a small town, her smile took them to a golden coast, where a slash of light from an ordinary sunset was suddenly different. He saw that smile and was about to say something.

But she spoke again. 'I got on the wrong coach, a year ago, discovered this town, and haven't found the momentum to leave.'

It was an unexpected revelation, one he could not find a response to, so he wriggled deeper into the loose ground he felt under the sheet, and listened.

'I had travelled for months, coach to train to train to coach.' Her voice settled, and was suddenly contained, no longer reverberant, held by soft dune vegetation around her. She gathered her skirt into a cocoon and squatted. One hand reached out to the fire. 'Finally, I thought to come across. There's only one passenger train that does that, once a week—across the desert. It brought me here.' She paused, not raising her eyes. 'Now, I'm kind of hankering to get on the road again.'

He still had not said a word.

'You know? You can stay still for so long, and then the desire to move gets you.'

He understood that desire.

'You want to be travelling again.' She fluttered long fingers. 'But in a year, I've gathered ... accumulated too much stuff. I'd have to ... I don't know.'

'No one likes getting rid of *stuff.*' He felt a catch in his throat. He'd never said anything truer.

Startled at his voice, as if she'd sat there alone a long time, peering into the flames of a fire she built herself, she looked up. 'Oh.'

'Does it have to be a road?'

She pulled a solemn face. 'How else can one travel?'

He thought of the foolishness of what he was about to suggest. She looked like a stray, a bronze figurine, a fire-toasted apricot. She could be none of those things. What did he know? She could be a harridan, a witch.

'I have a boat.' He hardly recognized his own voice. Hushed and contained by the dune behind him it sounded like his father's.

She tilted her head until her hair hung to one side, sweeping a cheek pinked by the heat of the fire. 'I don't know about boats.'

He laughed. 'No one does ... they're a thing unto themselves. I know because I have one.' His chest inflated on a long breath. 'And it needs a sail mended, bilges pumped, woodwork sanded, a winch dismantled. That's what it needs. Now, what it *wants* is another thing.' He thought about what *Obsidian* wanted. She was moored two miles from there, tugging against her tethers like a black mare. He thought about what he wanted.

She shifted, curling her legs around her on the sand. She seemed to be contemplating something. Her lips stayed still; a straight thoughtful line. 'Hmm.'

No more cars came along the road. Darkness wrapped around them as the fire died. He prodded it with a long twig, threw a few more on top, where they hissed and blazed, curling into ashen powdery forms of themselves.

'When were you thinking of doing this? Leaving, I mean.' He knew his own plans for departure, but left them unsaid.

For a long time, she gazed at the small flames. Perhaps she didn't mean to answer. The sound of the incoming tide became more urgent. A coastal breeze was whipping up from the south. It would chill the beach, the town, everything around there by the morning.

'I think about leaving every day.' Her voice had softened so it was in tune with the surf, almost inaudible. 'Some day, I'll do it—pack, buy tickets ...' She looked toward the sound of the waves on sand. '... quit my job. Something will make me do it.'

'Or some*one*.' He regretted the words, but wondered if she had heard him. She did not look like there was anyone in her life. People like her were solitary, eremitic, self-contained. Taking out his battered hip flask, he held it in her direction.

Without asking what was in it, she reached out, unscrewed the thimble top and took a brief shallow sip. When she swallowed, she looked at the bottle mouth and tilted her head. 'My, my.'

She could distinguish between good whisky and any old brown paper wrapped bottle. His first thought returned.

She overtook it, chin up-thrust, like a bird swallowing a worm. Arm outstretched to hand back the flask, she levelled eyes at him. 'Room for one more?' She wasn't talking about sips from a flask.

'Ah—I must be crazy. I'm a lone yachtsman.'

Her eyes were opaque, serious. 'Perhaps you're neither of those things.'

For a long while, until the fire died and the sky brightened, they were immobile. The moon broke out from between banks of clouds. He'd never questioned being a lone yachtsman; did not know what would happen if it changed.

'It would be my first time.'

He understood what she meant. There were many first times in a person's life. He thought of all the things he'd done just once, and things he had never done. Many came to mind, and there had to be more. What he was about to do would be a first. 'Tuesday, I was thinking. I have a few jobs to do, errands to run, and supplies ...'

'Provisioning.' Without salutation, she walked up the dune and disappeared. The last thing he saw in the gloom was the hem of that skirt floating upward and away.

It took two days to set the boat to rights. Even scrubbing the planks between the lazaret lockers and pumping bilges by hand, pushing an awl fifty times along the perforated side of a sail and splicing the ends of two lines seemed like nothing. He stowed the genoa and spare foresail, oilskins and two jerry cans in the quarter berth, pushing lumpy and rigid shapes in until they did not push back. He unfolded and inspected the lee cloth he had never used. He wanted it shipshape by Monday night. It had to be perfect, perfect. He told himself he was preparing for a guest, but was not that delusional. He swallowed the lump in his throat.

By Monday night. Which was when she appeared, standing on the finger jetty, wispy hair blowing in a fresh westerly.

He stopped coiling a line, straightened, half expecting her to ask permission to come aboard.

She didn't speak. On either side of her legs stood a small wheeled suitcase and a large holdall. On her back, on top of a zipped canvas jacket, was a backpack made of yellow fabric.

'Hello.' What else could he say? There was never a moment he doubted she would appear.

'Tuesday starts at midnight.'

He looked at his watch. It was nine-thirty. Holding out a hand, he helped her clear the stanchion and fall like a feather to his deck. It took him seconds—like a feather, like a feather—to leap to the jetty and hand over her bags. 'You never asked where we might be sailing to.'

She pointed. 'Out there, I guess.'

He looked her up and down. Part of him had expected her to turn up in the floating skirt. All of him expected her the following day. She held out two brand new cookie tins. 'One each.'

'That's a lot of cookies.' He clambered down the companionway and fiddled with the gimbaled spirit stove. 'Tea, I think.'

She pulled off the backpack and handed down two rigid plastic triangles of sandwiches.

He looked at the labels. *Curried Egg. Chicken Mayonnaise.* How did she know? 'Good. I mean, thank you.' He pointed at the dinette table in the middle of the saloon, where a bottle of Dimple stood.

Three days later they lay to anchor off a busy port, watching harbour lights at night. She huddled in a blanket from the forward berth—which he had given her—on a lazaret bench, nursing an enamel mug of coffee. He was quite comfortable on one of the bench berths behind the lee cloth, which still smelled like a chandler shop.

Hair curtained her face. When occupied with some intricate or messy work, she hooked it back behind her ears. She massaged one wrist absentmindedly, looking out towards the shore lights. She'd get used to turning a winch with time.

He could never tell if she was happy or uncomfortable or regretful or glad she had come out on the boat with him. Turning to tighten a line, he realized something and stopped. Three days. *Three days.* Three days, and they didn't know each other's names. She was asleep when he radioed to report departure, and did not mention he had a passenger. Now, it seemed almost too late to say his name or ask for hers. Looking at the distant line of light, perpendicular wavy reflections in the black sea, seagulls congregating over a beach, he thought they might go on that way; strangers with nothing to call each other by.

In flowered shorts and loosely-knitted cotton sweater she kept out of his way, but he saw her observe how he wound winches, tightened lines, watched the compass, held the tiller.

'We'll move on south,' he said, wishing for her name to tag onto the end of sentences.

'Show me what to do. I'll stand watch ... watches, whatever, I mean. My share ... I mean ... perhaps every night?' What swam beneath the surface of what she said?

'Sure.' It would be good to sleep through a stretch of dark hours. There was nothing to hold him back. During the day they sailed, watching the ribbon of land, multi-coloured or grey, or yellow or black, depending on their distance, time of day, and weather. It came and went, faded and reappeared; careful, careful, he was, to distance the boat from the shallows as she bucked or swanned, leapt and heaved when the leeward wind tugged like a magnet, pushed like bulldozer.

Why does the wind figure so, in the lives of all of us?

'Because we use it,' she said, from the forward deck.

Had he said the words aloud? Perhaps not.

'Everything we use is a danger, Eric.'

He nodded, digesting what she said. When had he told her his name? She must have been through papers under the chart table.

He pulled the canvas hat off and made tea, standing in bare feet on duckboard he scrubbed and sanded not a week ago. He put a match to the spirit stove and swung at the knee, flexing with the movement of the boat. She was on deck, above his head, in bright sunshine, hair knotted back under a back-to-front baseball cap. He felt her correct course and slightly furl the jib. He knew his boat, and also knew from what he felt in the vessel's response that she had lied to him.

He knew everyone had reasons to lie, and those who said otherwise were lying too. His were lies of omission—and mostly to himself.

It would be my first time. He remembered her saying those words, near his fire, sitting on his khaki groundsheet. She had lied, or she meant something else, because he was starting to see—feel—that she knew her way around a forward deck, around a tiller, around holding her balance below, when the vessel heeled and she made her way forward, hatchway to heads. She knew about granting and receiving privacy, about the safety of tidiness, about catting the anchor. She used words like lee shore and cockpit and spar and forestay.

He listened to her above, rinsing out her underwear and t-shirts in a bucket, having asked how long before they went ashore for supplies and fresh water. She knew about frugality of shipboard life, sparing even with conversation. She understood companionable silence.

She pulled a finger down the chart and peered up and down, as if she knew what she saw. She correctly wound a line around a cleat without having to look at what she was doing.

I don't know about boats. She must have meant something else. She must have meant she did not know about the sense of getting on a boat, not that she did not know anything about sailing. He had to ask. But first, he had to find out her name.

22

The sound of her singing up there startled him. Deep, rich, contralto words reached him and he recognized the song. It would be dark soon, and they would heave to, spend the dark hours watching the distant glimmering shore. It cheered him that she was comfortable enough, happy enough, to sing. The words—some of them—floated down to him as he layered bread, ham, cheese, tomato, lettuce.

... until the sun goes down

... water

... midnight

... ebbtide

... the ocean

... shoreline

... midnight

... on a wave

Catches and snatches of her song ebbed and flowed. *Midnight.* And then there was silence as the sun went down. The world darkened. She came below and smiled when he handed her a plate. 'Here you are, Midnight.' He knew now that even if she gave him her name, a name, it might not be the real one. After all, what was real?

Copper she was, gleaming, when she made a clean dive after making sure the water was safe. She watched for stingrays before she went in; jellyfish, sharks. She noted the security of a deep little bay almost enclosed by black shoals. She shaded her eyes to look below the surface. 'It's clear.'

He motored in and out through an opening where golden seaweed swished one way then the other on the current. She swam a few strokes and was immediately back at the boarding ladder, reaching for her towel before she stepped over the transom.

'Too cold?'

'Too deep.'

He looked out toward the horizon. His swim was longer, wider, wet and cold. Back at the chart table, towelled down and invigorated, he slid a pencil over his ear, thinking of the course to take, and saw his faded name, the boat call sign, in his writing, on an old card pinned to the bulkhead. 'Ah.'

All other misconceptions slipped, knotting others in their place, like a bowline. Like a clove and two half hitches. Which he saw her tie before they moored at a jetty somewhere down south, when she swung two inflatable fenders over the port side. 'Someone taught you to do that,' he hazarded.

'Someone left-handed.' She went down the companionway.

Silence followed clattering of plates and knives. She stowed everything away, clean, before they went ashore. He stood on deck, looking out towards buildings, a road, small houses, the spire of an old church. 'Make fast the aft line,' she called up. 'I haven't checked it.'

They crossed a busy road and surveyed a small coastal village, where it would be easy getting fuel, water and supplies. She disappeared among the aisles of a grocery store.

For a while he waited near a rotating book stand. 'Midnight?' His voice felt strange. It was the only name he could call. A couple buying hats looked at him. It was not impatience. It was something else. He didn't want this to be a month full of nothing but loss.

She emerged, laid a blue credit card on the counter.

'No, no.'

'Yes, yes.' Pasta and cans of things like beans, tomatoes, corned beef, condensed soup, instant mashed potato, dried peas, and braised meat were piled in a trolley, with tissues, toilet paper and other care items for herself, among which a drum of sunscreen.

'Planning a long trip?' A joke might settle his mind.

Dark eyes turned to his. 'A voyage.'

He lowered a jerry can of fuel and drums of water from the jetty and she straightened them near the cockpit. They feasted on fresh fruit and yogurt. The mood of departure was already on deck, the sun already just above the boom, the lazy jack about to be relieved of the mainsail.

'Last berries before the long haul,' he said.

'Mm—last yogurt.'

'You didn't ask where we're bound.'

She pointed down the coast. 'That way, I guess.'

Looking at varnished boards between his feet, he envied her the ability to abandon herself to the whims of time and wind and time of day and whatever choices he made without consulting her. He knew where *he* was bound. She never asked.

'No trains, then? You said you didn't know about boats.'

'I don't know about skippers.'

He laughed, finished his berries and yogurt, took her bowl and went below to prepare for departure. Later, when leaving her to the watch, he thought it was the closest she'd come to a personal revelation.

The storm that tossed them about—a twist of newspaper in a bath of roiling water—left them exhausted, neither of them willing to admit apprehension, neither telling the other they should have waited another day, at least, at the village. They watched its black retreating back, its shrug, its dwindling power, under a quarter rainbow. It had lasted three hours at the most, from lunchtime to dinner, but it wreaked havoc on deck and below. A brilliant sunset sent rays that lengthened the mast's shadow out over the water, which still churned.

'That was not fun, skipper.'

'No damage to *Obsidian*.' He wanted to say it wasn't his doing, not his storm, but held the phrase like a lozenge, under his tongue. 'We survived, Midnight. I lost a winch, but nothing dramatic.' If only it was all he could lose.

She sighed at the disorder in the galley, and set things to rights. She handed him a mug of coffee at the end of it. 'A plastic wineglass cracked, a can of spaghetti sauce dented, a bag of dried peas scattered, pasta shells all over the place, and I can't find one rubber glove.'

'What about the Dimple?'

'The whisky's fine. Those crazy bottles are indestructible. How did you go?'

'Lost a line ... glad the dinghy was secure. We need a new padlock for the starboard lazaret. Can't find the red winch handle.'

'A floating one, bobbing away. That's sixty bucks down the ... ah, maelstrom.'

He looked over the edge of the mug. 'That wasn't the first storm you ever weathered.'

She returned the look. 'Look ...'

'Sorry. Just curious, that's all.'

She hooked hair behind an ear. 'Not used to it.' Her laugh was full of the taste of irony. 'I should be grateful for any attention. Glad you can see me *at all.*' Turning her back, she moved to the forward cabin and drew the leather curtain closed with a snap.

He prepared simple spaghetti bowls with sauce warmed up in a pan, whose handle was hot to the touch. He bore it; punishment for annoying her with seven-word sentences that were really questions.

She sang in the last of the sunlight, alone on deck. It was always the same song.

... midnight

... the ocean

... midnight

... ebbtide

... shoreline

'I listen when you sing.' He continued to replace the duckboard he lifted to check for water in the bilges after the storm.

'It's anger.'

When he looked up she stood over him, fists on hips, making him shift back. '*Anger*? It sounds a bit ... '

'Soothing? Well—I soothe me.'

'Anger.' He repeated his mystification.

'Hmm—bet you didn't know it's the only eternal emotion.' Hot irony filled the saloon.

He expected her to retreat to the forward berth and yank the curtain shut. But she stood there.

They listened to the quietening wind, a sunset wind, which would have them heave to and rest after the day's ordeal.

She turned and washed out spaghetti bowls.

In four days, they sighted the cape. Breathing deeply with the confidence of sailing in familiar waters, he battled the emotion of not wanting to end the journey. Arrival, this time, meant the loss of something significant. He looked toward the shore. Soon he would face what he was going there to face. But for now, the mood of the voyage was still with him. Voyage; he used her word. He stood and she took the tiller.

They always captured his heart and mind, those cliffs. He scanned grassed crests and rocky hollows, going below for binoculars and coming back to notice she sailed closer. The profile of chalk, granite, shale— white and grey and ochre—made the landscape look flattened, like a painting. The water was so deep he didn't mind how close she sailed.

From the shore a glint; a shard of light. Someone watched, with binoculars. He trained his to cliff and path. What he glimpsed did not cause surprise at first, no astonishment. That had yet to reach the pit of his stomach.

Pointing to where the reflection of lens in sunlight came from, he laughed. 'That could almost be you.' Through lenses, a multi-coloured skirt billowed, wispy hair flew.

'It is me.'

He laughed although he knew she wasn't joking. His stomach churned. Lenses did not lie.

By his side, she stood steady on the boards of his boat, and waved.

The figure on the cliff waved back.

'She's waving. She waved back.' He lifted a tentative hand.

'Mm—of course.'

With binoculars held to eyes, his voice was so low she might not even hear. 'Why here?'

There was no answer. She went below in the middle of a conversation. Not unusual. Not moody, exactly; her habits matched his.

There was no wheeled suitcase, nor a holdall, below. The yellow back-pack was gone. So was Midnight. How could it be? They were still out on the choppy bay, with the only jetty still about a mile east of where *Obsidian* sailed on, regardless of Eric's bafflement. She couldn't have gone overboard, luggage and all. The dinghy was still lashed to the forward deck, five inches shy of the hatch. She couldn't have plunged into grey waves; she didn't like deep water. It could be as cold as it liked, it could be. Only not deep. She said it. He heard her. She'd stood not two feet from him, dripping wet, holding a towel to her chest in that way she had, before she stepped over the transom.

'Midnight!' He pulled the curtain to the forward cabin open. It was dark. The genoa sail was an untidy mass on top of the unmade berth. There was no wheeled suitcase, no holdall.

... *midnight*

... *ebbtide*

That contralto voice above, just over where he stood.

Eric held his breath. 'Midnight?'

There was no response. But she rarely answered when he called.

He clambered up into the cockpit. 'Midnight!'

The deck was as deserted as when he sailed alone.

The reason he had to return to that jetty was not the only depressing aspect of his arrival. He missed her. Hah! A lone yachtsman, hell bent on a successful last cruise, lonely. Never would he have guessed, when *Obsidian* was new, years ago, that this would happen.

He'd spent a night riding anchor in the bay, fifty, perhaps eighty yards out from the jetty's end. He had pulled the cabin below apart and put it back together again, and found no trace of her. Nothing. Not a hairpin, or that baseball cap, or an odd sock, or perhaps an empty biscuit tin. The only thing he found was a blue credit card which he flipped onto the dinette table in frustration. Did he remember her look when she said *Yes, yes*, and paid for their supplies?

He stared at it for a long time, sitting on the bench berth, where his lee cloth was attached to hooks on the bulkhead. A credit card was all that was left. He picked it up and took it on deck, sharp sunlight making him blink. 'Yes, yes,' he said to the mast, whose metal steps cast shadows like angular spiders against the column of steel.

Wait, wait. The card would have her name on it. He couldn't make it out in the glare. In the cockpit under the Bimini shade, he had to read the name twice. His name. His name on a blue credit card he had only seen once before. 'No.'

'Tell me how this can be,' he said later, to a woman behind a counter at the bank.

She looked at him through horned spectacles and gave a patient smile. 'It can be, sir, because it's yours.' She checked address, date of birth, other details and he stood there, perplexed. Mystified and nonplussed at the amount of money on the card.

'Is that credit ... debit ... what is it? Is it money I owe the bank?'

29

'Mr uh ... Havard. Eric ... it's your money. The account is in credit. In the black. Do you remember the PIN?' She had to ask it twice. Then get him to create a new number. It was a lot of money. Surely he remembered it was his? But she'd seen stranger things from behind that counter.

The next place he walked into was a dark brown pub, where the smell of beer and whatever it was they rinsed the tap lines with filled the deserted space. He sat in front of a glass holding two inches of Dimple, which he paid for with the card.

Next was the broker who had *Obsidian* up for sale in the window. 'Already,' he said to his reflection in the glass.

'Hey, Eric! You're back. I've had some interest in the ...'

He held up a hand. 'No. No—no longer for sale. I don't have to sell her. Take it down. Please.' He pointed at the window. 'She's not for sale.'

'But you said ... you said *this month*. That when you returned ...'

'I know what I said.' He shook his head. Looked at his hands on the counter. 'I know what I said. Something's happened. Don't ask me what —I can't explain.' He took a breath. 'She's not for sale.' A sudden feeling of lightness came over the length of him, feet to head, head to feet. It was the sensation of reprieve; release from the constriction of having to sell *Obsidian*. She was still his. 'It was not a farewell voyage after all.' His voice had that tone to it again, contained, unperturbed, like his father's.

Night fell early that day. Strapping the dinghy forward of the mast gave him a feeling he couldn't define, but he was not examining things too closely. He knew Midnight and the money were connected, but he had no idea how. He looked toward the cliffs and saw them become vaguer in the gloom. A necklace of lights came on in the distance, and a bank of cloud brought the horizon closer and closer.

He stayed up. It was like it was before; he and the Dimple bottle, he and the cockpit, he and the restless sound of the sea against the side. Slap. Slap. He stayed up and made instant mashed potato and canned corned beef. He pushed through fatigue and bafflement at the fortune that befell him. He felt his second wind when the moon emerged from behind a curved shimmer of light-edged cloud. He tugged on two lines, looked straight up along the mast to Sirius, high overhead. He released the tiller, watched the foresail flap and fill.

... midnight

... shoreline

... on a wave

... midnight

The contralto voice came from the top of his head, from the core of his spine. The cliffs faded into the distance. A shimmer caught his eye. What looked like a small campfire glowed at the foot of the distant cliff.

'Midnight!' He called. His voice wafted around, like a flight of night seagulls seeking light. It was much too far away. He couldn't trust his eyes. She was a wraith, thin but hardy and bendy like a bough. He knew he would never see her again.

He waved.

And she waved back.

TWO FUNERALS

BY SUE BRENNAN

So in Death, as in Life,

She will find her way to Him

Nellie looked at what she'd written, satisfied. The capitalisation of 'D' and 'L' had been a good idea, occurring to her as she brushed her teeth before bed, mulling it over. It added gravitas. Above the text would be a picture of her mother—the one when she was a missionary in the Philippines before Nellie's birth. In the picture, her mother was smiling with her eyes half-closed, as though waking from a pleasant dream. She was actually standing at the end of a row of six fellow missionaries. In the centre stood a priest. Of course, none of those people would be in the picture. The woman from the funeral home said she'd crop them out. The other thing Nellie liked about what she'd written was that most people would think *Him* referred to God. That was fine. To Nellie, though, it referred to her father, Lawrence Daniel Kerr, of whom she had no memory.

The Requiem Mass was well attended. The casket was stacked with wreaths of lilies, carnations, and roses which would later be given to the hospital. In the vestibule, was a donation tin for the cancer research foundation. Nellie's mother had been a vital force in the community until her protracted battle with ovarian cancer had finally put an end to her. Bishop Rossi himself presided and spoke of her with deep admiration. Beside Nellie in the front pew were her aunts, uncles and cousins, quietly sniffling. Behind them, the mostly elderly congregation sang along in tremulous voices the hymns chosen by her mother: *Make me a Channel of Your Peace* and *Softly and Tenderly Jesus is Calling*. Nellie wanted to sing but could not due to the tightness in her throat. At the appointed time, she stepped out of her seat, genuflected, and proceeded to the pulpit.

'My mother,' she read, 'was a good woman. I don't know anyone who'd say otherwise. It is well known that she spent her youth serving the Lord, spreading His Word, in Uganda, Sri Lanka, China, and, finally, the Philippines. It was there, relatively late in life, that she met my father and had me, so that put an end to that.'

The congregation laughed, gently, as she hoped they would.

'And yet it didn't,' she continued and told them what they already knew: her mother, tragically widowed after one year of marriage, moved back to her hometown at the behest of *her* mother, updated her teaching certification and taught mathematics and religious education at St Joseph's until her retirement.

'Barely a week goes by,' Nellie said, 'that I don't get someone coming up to me in the supermarket, saying, *oh, you're Mrs Kerr's daughter. She was my favourite teacher.*'

When this happened, Nellie always graciously accepted the compliment and said she'd pass it on.

'Mum,' she'd say. 'I saw one of your old students today.'

Her mother would insist upon knowing what they looked like, how old they seemed, trying to place them. She'd long since given up on Nellie getting any of their names.

Nellie looked up at her aunts.

This is not the time, their expressions compelled her. *Go on with what you've written.*

'Upon her retirement, Mum threw herself into her work with the St Vincent de Paul Society, the Catholic Women's League, and the Liturgy Committee. I see familiar faces here now, other members of those worthwhile organisations.'

Again, Nellie looked at her aunts.

'Today we commend the soul of Elizabeth Mary Kerr unto the Lord,' she said, choking over her mother's name. 'A mother, a daughter, a sister and aunt, a friend and colleague. A child of God.'

She bowed her head, put the paper in her pocket and returned to her seat, wondering if anyone had noticed her omission of *a wife*.

After the interment—a gathering of those twenty or so besides family who believed Elizabeth Kerr was nothing short of a saint—they made their way to a modest red-brick house. It was here that Nellie had lived all of her life yet she did not call it home. Her mother had always called it Gran and Gramps' house, and until she was six, she and her mother had shared the same bedroom.

She'd always said, 'One day we'll get our own place, Nellie.'

Realising, perhaps, that their daughter and granddaughter were never going to leave, Nellie's grandparents had built an extension.

Nellie and her aunts immediately set about heating up food and peeling cling film from the platters prepared earlier. The cousins welcomed guests into the house and made them comfortable. The uncles, similar in their dislike for small-talk, stood outside with bottles of beer and loosened ties. Over the next three hours, Nellie was asked several times what she was going to do with the house. Would she continue to live there? She couldn't see any reason why not but replied that she hadn't given it much thought. Her aunts had advised her not to rush into anything.

'Not many people your age get to own their own house,' they'd said.

Nellie was twenty-three and had two colleagues her age who'd taken advantage of the first-home owners grant and locked themselves into heavy mortgages.

'It's nothing much to look at,' her aunts conceded. 'You might want to do some renovations. Put your own stamp on it.'

It had a blankness that went beyond austere. After her grandparents had died—they were gone within two years of each other when Nellie was a young teen—her mother had decluttered it entirely. Gone from the walls were the long-stitch tapestries of English cottages. Gone were the Staffordshire dog figurines that guarded each door. Gone were the laughing pig salt and pepper shakers. No more dishes of potpourri on the side tables. Her mother had moved into her parents' room and removed everything but the bed, wardrobe, and nightstand, on which a well-worn copy of the Catholic Book of Prayers rested until the day she died. As Nellie moved into her teens, she put up posters of Rob Lowe, Andrew McCarthy and Christian Slater, because that's what she'd seen her friends do. Nellie had stared at the long-haired, bright-eyed men and thought, *Who are you? What are you doing in my room?* Her mother permitted the posters but insisted that the door be kept closed.

Nellie was also asked by many guests to stand in front of the defunct fireplace in the living room. Above it hung a photograph of her father— one of two photographs she'd seen of him.

'Good heavens,' they exclaimed as she stood there. 'It's uncanny.'

And it was: he was tall, gangly, and so was she; he had a square jaw and wide mouth, and so did she. His hair was thick, straight and dark, parted on the side. She'd experimented with bobs and perms but eventually settled on a blunt, short cut that she parted on the side. It was more Gertrude Stein than the Audrey Hepburn she'd been aiming for. In the photo, he smiled. She was not smiling, standing there before them.

'You're even wearing the same thing,' they noted. 'Kind of.'

He wore a black suit and an open-collared white shirt. She wore black pants and a dark green shirt over a white T-shirt.

Some asked tentatively, 'You never knew him, is that right?'

'Correct,' she said and, satisfied, they allowed her to leave.

She found that there was a lot to do in the kitchen before being hustled out by a close friend of the family.

'It's not the time for that now,' they said. 'You need to be out there. Don't be odd.'

Chastised, Nellie, sat between her aunts and cousins, half-listening to them talk about the preparations for Easter, which her mother had always been involved in. Her aunts weren't in the same league as Nellie's mother—they'd been concerned about their younger sister's missionary zeal—but they were obstinately Catholic. She glanced at her father's photo, imagining what it would feel like to have her hand enveloped in his as they walked to the park, or to have him read her a story as she sat in his lap. Childish desires that had never waned.

'I see the resemblance now,' someone sitting across from her said. 'With all of you together. The eyes. It's the blue eyes.'

'Yes,' one of the aunts said. 'All of us have the Kilkeary eyes. Nellie was lucky to not get the ears as well.'

Laughter.

She shifted in her seat and cleared her throat, and her aunts—sensing her readiness to flee—each put a hand on her thigh.

***

When she was ten, being adopted was suddenly the worst thing imaginable. Perhaps the concept was too bizarre for a bunch of privileged, suburban, Catholic children from large families to comprehend. They ran around the schoolyard in packs, accusing kids they didn't like of being adopted—kids who'd wet their pants in the second grade, who still couldn't do cursive writing, who weren't good at sport, kids who had many freckles.

'Your father's dead,' they said, sneering at Nellie.

'I *know*, stupid,' she said. 'So?'

On this particular day, she'd come to school with a bad cold. Her nose had been dripping and she'd wiped it on her sleeve. Someone had seen her and now she was prey.

'I saw your mum,' one of them said. 'That's not your mum. She'd old. That's your granny.'

'No, that's her mum,' one of them corrected. 'Her mum's old.'

'So what?' Nellie said. Her head was throbbing.

'You're adopted,' they said. 'You don't look anything like her.'

Nellie realised that was absolutely true. By the time she got home, she was convinced and asked her mother, who treated it as *a silly question*. Many of Nellie's questions were silly.

'Why don't I look like you then?'

She was pulled into the bathroom and made to stand on the bathtub.

'Look at us here in the mirror,' her mother said and smoothed her hair. 'Just look at us.'

Apart from the blue eyes they also both had light brown hair that turned almost blond in summer. As Nellie got older, her hair would darken, but she didn't know that then. It was enough; same eyes, same hair. She was her mother's child. But *something* was wrong. She felt it and, being unable to articulate it, became disagreeable—talking back to adults, getting into fights at school, flouncing about with dramatic sighs.

One evening, she overheard her grandmother and mother talking. Nellie had just finished her bath. The TV was on and her grandfather snored.

'She's turning into a brat,' her grandmother said.

'All children go through this,' said her mother.

'You and your sisters didn't.'

'Leave it, Mum. I just want to watch the telly.'

'She's a sensitive one. Why don't you just tell her?'

'Mum, no. Leave it, will you?'

'It wasn't your fault,' her grandmother said.

'I can't,' her mother said loudly, tearfully. 'I can't.'

'Oh, Lizzy...'

Nellie burst into the room, demanding to know what her mother should tell her and was sent to bed. That weekend, the aunts were brought in. They had five children between them, so. They asked Nellie what was on her mind and, confused, she repeated the adoption fear.

'Lord, no,' they said. 'You're a Kilkeary *and* a Kerr. Rest easy on that.'

'What was Grandma talking about?'

There was a long silent minute before one of them said, 'Your dad may be alive. The thing is...he disappeared.'

'What?' Nellie asked, startled, looking around the room as though he might be hiding behind the curtains.

They explained that shortly after Nellie was born, he'd gotten a call from Scotland that his brother was very ill. They'd been close and everyone urged him to go home. Money was scarce but it was found and off he went.

'We know he arrived in Scotland,' one of the aunts, the older one, said. 'Because he called saying the brother had died. Then there was another call. He'd be staying on a while to help out. Your mum wrote letters and sent photographs of you. Now, sweetie—none of us ever saw the letter that your mum got. We only know what she eventually told us. He was very sorry but he wasn't coming back to Australia.'

'Why not?' Nellie asked.

'We don't know,' the aunt said sadly. 'It was a terrible thing to do. He'll have had his reasons. But he'll also have God to answer to.'

'But they were married. He *had* to.'

'People don't always do what they promise to do,' the aunt said, which, for ten-year-old Nellie, was incomprehensible.

'Your mum, obviously, was distraught—'

'—she was a wreck, is what she was—'

'—and so you ended up living here with Gran and Grandpa.'

They stopped talking to allow Nellie to cry. They waited for questions, but Nellie was unable to formulate anything beyond *where?* and *why?*

'Your mum has done an amazing job, hasn't she?' the younger aunt said, rubbing Nellie's back. 'She's a teacher, and she's on all those committees, and she takes good care of you...and you've got us! She's doing her best, darling, but she can't talk about this. I guess it still hurts too much. She'll tell you in her own words. In her own time.'

But she never did, she never did, and Nellie didn't ask.

***

It was unconscionable that no one had even offered to pick her up. Getting from Sydney to Edinburgh on short notice had been no easy feat —a 25-hour flight with a 3-hour layover in Doha, and close to $3000. She wheeled her suitcase along Princes Street, bleary-eyed and numb with fatigue but thrilled to see a castle looming right there in the middle of the city. The bed and breakfast was difficult to find given that all the houses and streets looked much the same—rows upon rows of three-storey sandstone townhouses fenced with black wrought iron. When she saw the discreet sign above the green door, she almost swore aloud with relief.

Her half-sister, Freya, had recommended it because it was located near to where she lived.

'You'll be able to pop round as soon as you've freshened up,' she'd emailed.

What Nellie really wanted was a cup of tea, a shower and a nap. She removed her clothes from the suitcase, laid them out on the bed and pressed her fingers around her eye sockets and temples, trying to ward off the incipient headache.

'I've arrived in Edinburgh,' she texted to Alex, even though Alex had made it clear texts from her were no longer welcome.

'I'm okay,' she added and went to the bathroom. When she emerged, she felt marginally revived. The navy linen skirt suit which she trotted out whenever she needed to look 'smart' made her appear frumpy. She hadn't had time to get her hair done and considered plucking out the more noticeable white hairs that sprang from the crown of her head. The lipstick—Dior #453 *Adorée*—was an extravagance she couldn't afford at $40, but during the layover, she'd gotten caught up in the glamour of duty-free shopping and her first international flight. The deep crimson shade made her look sickly and older than her fifty-five years, but she was too tired to care. Anyway, as far as she could tell, it was only Freya who had any interest in meeting her.

The address she'd been given was three blocks away, so she dawdled along the quiet streets, incapable of complex thought.

It sure is different here, was all she could think.

She slowed to a standstill when she approached the address she'd been given. There was a van parked out front. Three people in black and white lifted trays from the back of it, carried them up the stairs and disappeared inside. She edged closer and the three people came out, retrieved more trays and went inside again. Quickening her pace to that of a passerby on their way somewhere, she did a quick look left at the side of the van and a quick look right into the house, ascertaining two things: the reception was being catered for by Evan's Fine Foods & Caterers, and the house's foyer was inhospitably dark.

At the end of the street, she feigned interest in the clouds and looked back. A long black car, almost limousine-like in appearance, stopped alongside the van. She counted six people emerge and gather in a group on the pavement before ascending the stairs. Mourners returned from the cemetery, she expected. Freya had said the house would be open to receive guests from 3 pm. It was now 2:35 pm. The thought of lingering outside was as appealing as arriving early, so she headed on around the corner. She was pleasantly surprised to find a pub with seats outside populated by young people talking quietly, looking at their phones, with pints of dark amber beer in front of them. She went inside, ordered a glass of white wine on a whim and seated herself by a window.

Again, all she could think as she looked around the pub was, *it's different*.

The wine was sour but cheap and in a large glass. She swallowed two paracetamol tablets in two gulps. Her sleep-deprived, jet-lagged mind became looser, more free-wheeling as she drank. Had this been her father's local, she wondered. Had everyone called out, *Hey Larry*, when he walked in? Freya wrote that he was, though reticent, well-liked. Did he have a paunch, Nellie mused, and the red nose of a heavy drinker before the strokes laid waste to him?

Nellie was appreciative of Freya's willingness to talk about their father. She would have to remember to tell her. She'd written it in an email, but it would be nice to tell her face to face. There'd not been a peep from the other two, Colin and Lorna, and Nellie got the sense that Freya, the youngest, wasn't close to either of them. Their mother, like Nellie's, had died of cancer, breast cancer, some time ago.

'Losing a parent, even as an adult, leaves one, to a degree, feeling orphaned,' Freya had written, and Nellie agreed. To an extent. The absence of her mother had been something she'd experienced even while she was still alive. Even when they were in the same room, her mother was always preoccupied, never fully *there*. After her death, Nellie ransacked the house and garage and found letters that had been returned. Letters accompanied by photographs of toddler-Nellie, first-day-at-school Nellie. Pages of her mother's neat handwriting entreating her husband to come home. Nellie, then, had written a letter to the address in Dundee and received it, four months later.

Not at this address, someone had written in red ink, and that was that until the internet appeared and turned the world inside out.

Feeling maudlin and a little drunk, she reluctantly stood. It was 3:10 pm and she'd been awake for almost 38 hours.

The street was lined with cars and the catering van was gone. The door was open, so she stepped inside. It was a small area for the removal and storage of hats, coats and shoes. To her left was a staircase with a gleaming rosewood balustrade and carpeted stairs. The room to her right was filled with people, quietly talking and holding glasses of wine. Above them, between them, she could see an enormous mirror, paintings and photographs on the walls, and large flourishing potted palms in the corners. She swallowed. Many of the people were elderly. The less robust were seated on the plush sofa and chairs in the bay window. There were several wheelchairs and walking frames. This was, after all, the funeral reception for a ninety-three-year-old man. A waiter came through with a tray of small quiches. Nellie took two and, following in the waiter's wake, entered the room.

The few she made eye contact with gave her a nod, but mostly she was ignored. She ate the quiches while she looked at the photographs on the mantle and saw evidence, though it wasn't needed, that she was, indeed, a Kerr. Three or four generations were on display. Faded black and white photographs with stern-looking folk alongside glossy colour photos of ecstatic children at Euro Disney.

At the far end of the room, a young man stood by a table with overturned glasses and various bottles.

'Wine, ma'am?' he asked. 'Beer? Soft drink?'

'Wine, please,' Nellie said. 'White.'

With this in hand, she moved on to the back of the house, also crowded. There was a dining table that could seat twelve. Food was laid out there and catering staff bustled around the large, well-equipped kitchen adding more to it. It was a feast. Through the glass doors, she saw even more people in the garden. One group of three, in particular, was familiar. They were tall and long-limbed, like Nellie, but stood poised, confident, in their element. They were in harmony with the manicured garden beds and topiary trees lining the stone walls; in fact, everyone here seemed to match the decor and each other. Nellie felt out of place. Singular.

And now it was a matter of going out and introducing herself to them, to Freya. She drank her wine and observed. Colin was doing most of the talking and seemed to be laying down the law. Lots of gesticulations: no; that's the end of it; I won't hear another word; I've already told you this.

Freya looked towards the house, squinting, covering her eyes. Lorna moved very little, other than to touch her face, her hair. Perhaps she was murmuring.

It was too hostile out there, Nellie decided and asked for another wine. Despite the time she'd had to think about it, she had no idea what she wanted to say to them. She wasn't here on a fact-finding mission—she and Freya had already communicated to each other as much as they knew, or so she believed.

Lawrence Kerr had never mentioned a wife and daughter in Australia. Never. Freya had politely requested proof initially—not a DNA test, nothing as sordid as that—but a photograph, perhaps? A letter? Nellie had photographed the envelopes that had been returned from Dundee, as well as the picture of her father that hung in the living room. And then, of course, there was herself. Exhibit A. The address in Dundee, it turned out, was his childhood home. Colin, Lorna and Freya had fond memories of summer holidays there. By the time Nellie had located Freya Davids (nee Kerr), their father was in a vegetative state, and that may have allayed any fears they had of Nellie intruding upon their family, seeking a relationship. Freya had also been clear that their father had been a kind man but not a clever one. After his wife's death, still grieving, he'd been targeted by a conniving woman and remarried within a year. She'd spent the lot and left after his first stroke. Freya wanted Nellie to understand there was no inheritance, not for any of them.

Nellie manoeuvred her way through the living room to the foyer. A line of teenagers and children filed down the staircase. Some of them went out the front door, and some came into the living room seeking food and parents. On a bureau by the door, was an open book. People had written their condolences to the family. It must've been brought over from the funeral home because there were pages and pages of signatures and messages.

'So sorry for your loss,' she wrote. 'Eleanor Marie Kerr.'

Once it was written, she realised that she did not, in fact, need to speak to Colin, Lorna or Freya. They hadn't welcomed her into the family. Freya, the spokesperson, had inquired very little into Nellie's life, and yet she knew a great deal about hers—her children, her renovations, her difficult-but-rewarding career, her health scare.

She drained her glass and placed it firmly on the bureau, causing the man nearby to look over curiously, then with disapproval.

'What?' Nellie said.

He raised his eyebrows and looked back towards the woman he was with.

Nellie tapped the cover of the condolences book which was inscribed in gold lettering: Craigmillar Castle Park.

'Is this where the cemetery is?' she asked him. 'Excuse me, is this where—'

'Yes, it is,' he said, clearly displeased. 'Are you family?'

'Are you?' she asked.

His jaw dropped open and he turned to his scowling lady friend. Nellie had no idea why she took such pleasure in their discomfort.

She went outside and onto the pavement intent on finding a taxi. If she were savvier, she'd have an Uber app, but she wasn't, so she walked. After a while, she neared a crossroad with a steady stream of traffic, and, closer, a Sainsbury's. Her instincts were right—on a side street next to the supermarket was a taxi rank. When she told the driver where she wanted to go, he warned her it was a fair way and would cost a bit.

'In for a penny, in for a pound,' she said and settled into the back seat.

It was almost 4 pm. She was incapable of doing the mathematical calculation necessary to know what time it was in Australia and took out her phone. There was a text from Alex.

'Nels,' she read and winced at the endearment. 'Hope it works out but... please don't. Please stop.'

Nellie knew this meant please stop texting, and for the next thirty minutes hardly noticed the drive past grand private homes into ugly newer suburbs.

'You and your mother worship,' she recalled Alex telling her. 'She basically neglected you, you know, and you demand this...this fucking love from everyone.'

Of course, this would only sent Nellie into a sulk and then a rage.

'Why not love me then?' she'd scream. 'Is that so hard?'

To end it, Alex recited all the horrible things Nellie had said and done during their relationship. It was the way it always went, but Nellie would only remember the kindness, the affection, the attention, that each new partner bestowed on her in the beginning.

Suddenly, they were stopped in front of another castle—a blocky, grey and uninviting building.

The guard at the gate encouraged her to take a glossy brochure of the castle grounds and pointed her in the direction of her recently buried father. It was, ironically, easy to find. There was an older grave next to his, that of Rose Delores Kerr nee Madigan 1946 -1999. Nellie gave it no mind. She opened out the brochure, spread it on the ground and sat.

'Hello, you old goat,' she said softly, fingering the white and pink petals of an unfamiliar flower. 'I have something for you.'

From her handbag, she removed her wallet. Tucked into the zippered purse was a small envelope containing her mother's hair. Nellie had snipped this as her mother lay watching *Law and Order* on the TV above the hospital bed.

'What's that for?' her mother had asked, and Nellie had shrugged.

The hair was fine and white, with a slight curl. This was the first time she'd touched it since she'd taken it. It had no smell. She pushed it rudely into the soil.

'There,' she said.

PERFECTLY FORMED

SHORTLISTED STORIES:

DISOWNMENT

BY CAROLINE JAMES MACKIE

I WANT TO TELL ABOUT ME, AND ABOUT HOW I WAS AFFECTED BY what happened to me. I think it could make a difference to someone out there that might recognise even the slightest similarity to their own 'story'. Because we all have a story, don't we? This is mine.

It's the fact, the very *fact*, that they'd even thought so badly of me. I was their only child! I was only up Saughton for 8 weeks, no time off! They knew this. I would be coming home soon and we'd sort things out. They never even visited me! You don't suddenly become a career criminal because they put you in with a few lowlifes for the old short, sharp, shock, eh? Like, you get a crash course or something.

I remember I'd told mum before I even went to court that it was going to be okay, and not to worry. Like she was worried... at all? She had seemed worried. In hindsight, probably only because of the 'shame' of it all. Or that I'd get off with it. What happens? Couldn't believe it myself, but I got 'sent down'... as they say. Then they disowned me.

Literally, disowned me, via an official lawyer's letter, two days before I'm to get out. Told me my stuff was in boxes in the shed now and to call first before collecting it. There was even a time limit on when I had to have it collected, before it all got dumped! My room was now a sewing room and a home gym! Well that was fast! It's like, they couldn't wait to get rid of me and had had it all planned already.

'... cannot be associated with criminals... dad can't show his face in the pub... Mrs Peterson (Mrs fucking Peterson!) said she's watching and will call the police the minute...' I have the letter still. I try not to look at it too often. If you're reading this, try and put yourself in my place. How hurt would you be? I honestly just thought it would blow over. I obviously never really understood the implications of being 'disowned'. It took a while.

So anyway, my sentencing was for non-payment of parking fines. Parking fines! I didn't even have a car anymore as I had written it off just before my court date. It was a lot of money, sure and I hold my hands up, it's all true, I was a thoughtless, teenaged waster that didn't give a rat's arse. Mum wouldn't even allow dad to lend me it though the first time, so I never asked again. Then I just kept getting fines upon fines and just parked anywhere I liked so got more on top of those. Dad had wanted to help; I know he did. They both also knew I was unemployed, again. Gimme a break though! I wasn't a criminal! I could still get a new start at Halfords or somewhere! I needed to get a job and of course I'd get one, if only to save up for a better car. It all fell on deaf ears though. They'd given me so many chances, blablabla, I was nothing but a no-user, would never amount to anything, why hadn't I gone to university, because I was stupid blablafuckinbla. That was some ripping I got.

Then came my accident, my arrest, my sentencing... and my payback was disownment. I still can't get my head around them doing that and wonder that I hadn't perceived any huge dislike from either of them before then? Thirty five years later and the mind still boggles.

That's another thing, it was dad's old car that I totalled, and they'd been 'fond' of it... I ask you!... It was a car! I'm their son, but they cried more about that car than me and my broken leg, which of course I had to hobble about on in the jail until the cast came off! It is of course, also how they caught up with me for those unpaid fines. I was counting my blessings (when I came round in hospital) that I only had a broken leg. The car had done a couple of summersaults and landed on the edge of a ditch - I honestly thought I'd died and it was bloody lucky no-one else did - they'd had to cut me out of it. I don't really remember much.

Then I'd had to lie listening to my parents going on about the car upholstery being ruined (so sorry for bleeding!) and how they hadn't even been allowed to get the picnic blanket out of the boot before the yard crushed what was left of it all into a cubic metre of scrap. I didn't tell them I'd tossed the blanket months before as it smelled mouldy and disgusting, and yet they were mourning it! Then the police officers came in and they were so scandalised, they didn't even hang around to bring me home. I was to be done for possession too... slightly too much weed in my pockets so that was a huge nail in my coffin as far as my parents were concerned. That was eventually dropped as it was clearly for personal use and they considered I'd suffered enough. From hospital though, I was immediately incarcerated, no bail... and, basically, that was that!

She'd always been a stickler, Mum. I remember that much. Mrs f'n Peterson up the road hadn't helped mind you. I do wonder if mum was unduly influenced after moving there as I have no recollection of any miserable childhood before then. Nothing that really stands out. I got pocket money; I got presents at appropriate times. Dad took me places. As I got older, I vowed to shove one of that Mrs P's dahlias up her hole one of those days. Bint. Never liked me the minute she first laid eyes on me (I was eight!) and it all went downhill from there. Mum of course worshipped the ground she reigned over (the whole allotment!) and wouldn't hear a word against her, but that woman had far too much to say about our family life, and me in general. Mum was always saying stuff like 'Mrs Peterson says she saw you smoking yesterday!' (mild whack across the head before I could deny, although she probably *had* seen me and I was just happy she hadn't realised it was dope) and 'Mrs Peterson says you need to stand up and not slouch so much,' (rough yank to my shoulders as I passed her in the hall). 'Mrs Peterson says your results are a scandal!' (like I cared what Mrs Fuckface P said!) Dad would just shake his head at me every time. He really was no hero, no role model at all.

I suppose it didn't help that I ran over the woman's cat with my new bike. By accident! I actually had never liked the hateful, flea-bitten animal and it didn't like me either. Yes, I had fired off a few pellets at it over the years, but I had NOT intended to kill it. The mess alone! The drama! I got hurt too, by the way... stupid animal darting out like that, I went arse over elbow and had scrapes and bruises for weeks. I did get a fright seeing it lying there too, obviously potted... eyes lying next to its head was a good clue. I was upset! My new bike was all bent wheels and bits of cat! Did anyone comfort me? No! I was a veritable pariah in the cul-de-sac for ages! That had been a few years previous and no amount of apologising made Mrs P (or mum for that matter) believe it had been an accident. I was raking leaves and emptying bins for my sins for months after, until I just refused to do it anymore. That didn't go down very well either, come to think of it. Man, I had it going for me, didn't I?!

Also, had only come home drunk a few times really, last time only shortly before the accident. Nothing had even been said about it! Might have been the catalyst? Who knows, I was never informed, but it's safe to assume. There was also that time I had a party when they were away one weekend, but it hardly counts for much... surely? Minimal break-ages; not that much of their Christmas booze stash drunk. I was fifteen for god's sake and basically just showing off to older kids. That's just normal, no? Did it have to count at all, in the grand scheme of things? It was four years before the accident, followed by the prison fiasco! But yes, apparently, all my misdemeanours led to my final banishment. My time in jail gave them the incentive to 'cut the chord' properly, finally, easily. I made it fuckin easy for them.

I should have seen it coming, I suppose. Getting chucked out at the very least. They hadn't been too chuffed when I had come home telling them I couldn't pay next month's dig money as I'd been laid off. I hadn't expanded upon why and honestly, it wasn't my fault! The place had closed down! Had also caused me to come home drunk that few days before, eejit, just hadn't told them yet. And that's another thing actu-ally... not one of my pals ever had to pay dig money and I was miffed that I had to and told them so... huge argument of course!

So then what? I was homeless, patently. Well, fuck 'em. And fuck Mrs Peterson. I'd trample her flowers yet! Dad was so spineless, he wouldn't have had a say, I'm sure.

I remember wondering if they had found my stash. I had been looking forward to a wee joint as soon as I got home and was gutted when that all fell through. My priorities were a bit skewwhiff and being disowned bothered me way less than losing my stash. I figured they couldn't have found it or it would have been mentioned, but prayed it was just in amongst my things! And my books. And all my gear. They had better not have damaged my skateboard! And I needed my bike now, so I had to go and get it all soon. Fuuuuck. Could they not have, like, given me notice? Let me find a place first? I had of course assumed I was going 'home' when I got out, Now how was I...? Ooooh, I could have spit. Bloody mum. And I just knew that Mrs Fuckerson had had a hand in it. I honestly had other things to consider, more than my 'disownment' and at the time, well, sure it hurt, but perhaps not as it should have. I didn't really understand it. Just knew I wasn't welcome at my parents' house anymore. Lots of teenagers get chucked out, so it was actually years before it properly registered. They'd disowned me!

When I look back on that time of my life, I can only shake my head. What was I like!? What a daft kid. Really. But still a kid. Still a kid for sure. A spoiled kid, mind, despite then being disowned. Only nineteen. Maybe old enough to be less of a screw-up by then but come on... only nineteen. I'd needed that wake-up call really, but in full hindsight, it was the wrong way to go about it. I didn't deserve to be disowned for goodness sake!

Not that I would ever have told them that, about it being a wake-up call, sort of - they did still let me down in a major way, after all. I had a pretty tough time of it for the few months before I sorted myself out. Plenty had it worse, but I was alone and felt really abandoned, fresh out of prison. I felt really hard done by and had a lot of anger, but I was scared, too. I swore even then that I'd never do anything like that to my kids if I had them. Never. That's not the way!

Nowadays, my children know about their grandparents, but *they* never knew their grandkids, and none of us attended their funerals which I only found out about after the fact each time. Just in the passing. Dad went first, probably henpecked to death, I don't really know. Mum, a few years after him, in an old folks' home by all accounts. I'm glad in a way she never got to infect my kids with her poison, but it hurts too. Sad really.

I got over them, but it needed therapy, many years after the fact. You realise, as you get older, stuff affects you! I forgive them now; they maybe had their own sorrows. I'll never know though. They didn't take the trouble to confide in me, their only family.

Anyway... I got my act together with a bit of help from decent folk that gave me the benefit of the doubt. I knew from day one in there, they'd never get me back in prison. Hateful bloody place, and the scare did work, have to say. Taught me the kind of guy I did not want to become and how to avoid all contact with any of them. For sure. I don't advocate it, not even a little bit, but I'm convinced it did 'sort' me. Mum and dad broke my heart, but their actions steeled me too. As well as gave me that shake to sort myself out. More that even prison did.

It wasn't easy, but after a period of couch surfing with mates, just to emphasise to me how much I hated such a life, I managed to get my new manager (at the skateboard shop I'd finally convinced to take me on) to vouch for me with the council, and I got a wee flat. My stuff had been long stored in his garage already. He'd even collected it for me, so I hadn't had to go there. He understood. He was a good guy; I owe him still. To be honest, I never ever visited mum and dad again. I just cut my losses and let them stew in it, although to be honest I was afraid to at first. I was also advised not to actually, by people with more compassion. It was their loss really. Sorry I was such a disappointment to you folks. HUH!

Of course, I never saw Mrs. P again either. Nor did I take any kind of revenge on her, although it was on the back burner for a while, believe you me. Common sense eventually made me realise she was just some poor deluded widow of a certain age who just didn't like kids. Mum obviously wasn't a widow, but had a soulmate in her, I'm thinking. Dad was just collateral damage. I hope they enjoyed their gym, their sewing room, and their stupid allotment. They missed so much over the years, and I still don't really know why. It's not like I was in line to inherit anything of particular value. They just wanted shot of me, clearly.

With regular money coming in, I had my wee flat looking nice before too long. I had talent for it and knew it. I still had the odd toke but didn't see the same crowd as before and had no old friends among my acquaintances then anyway. (I still roll the odd joint too! Nothing wrong with a bit of weed now and again.) I was by then staying in a part of town I never would have considered living in until the council offered me the flat so, it was all good. New life and all. It took me a while to save enough for a car, but my bike did well for me. I'd bought it with my own pocket money savings at aged sixteen - I even remember Mrs P's sneer when I cycled past her for the first time. If she'd known it would one day soon kill her stupid cat, I'm sure my tyres would have been slashed that first day. Anyway, by the time I had saved enough, it felt stupid to take on such a money-pit as a car, so I put it towards my own place instead.

That was my first. Then came a second, bigger place and I sold that on too after renovating it so I bought two small places and did the same again while living in a caravan on site. Bim, bam, boom, I'm now the CEO of a big property concern. My own. Almost too many places in this town to mention, and loads in towns around here, done up by me and my people. From dump to palace in no time. All mod cons to the highest standards. Most sold on for decent profit, some kept as reasonable rentals (and holiday lets) in a separate section of the business that my wife now handles to a very profitable degree. All using my employees or contractors.

Of course, I did the first one all myself, then a few more, but now it's all builders and plumbers and... well, all the trades. I'm the boss. I have a car now of course, as does my wife, and all the kids took their driving test before they left our lovely home here for uni. God, the place is empty now.

My wife says we should slow down, now that the kids are all away at university (all three of them, all doing great) and we should travel more. We can certainly afford it and we're still only in our early fifties. I've never had a lick of debt since those unpaid fines and to be fair, only had a couple of speeding penalties over the years and paid immediately. One of them was when racing home from a job to get there in time for our eldest being born, right in our own living room. That was three homes ago. The other two were born in the second one and we moved here when the eldest was six. I figure we're here for the duration.

I (we) have tried not to spoil our kids, although by some standards, they perhaps are pretty privileged. Well of course they are. They also know who to butter up when they want something and they usually end up getting it, but we make them work for it too. My wife's parents are lovely, hands-on-when-needed, grandparents and wonderful in-laws too, have to say. They're getting on now, and I feel truly blessed to have had them around for as long as I have. I consider myself a very lucky man, and do tell my wife so, regularly.

It seemed to work though, whatever we did bringing them up, however we did it, because despite the wild, unsanctioned parties (!) and the late, drunken nights and being little shits at regular intervals (no dead cats among them though), we've neither of us disowned any of them yet, not even for five minutes, and they are all great kids, very much to be proud of. If any of them had been working yet and staying at home, I'm here to say that dig money would have been involved! I do see the good in that now. But as they are even yet still at 'school', so to speak, it has never been an issue. We are very proud of all of them, especially my little princess who is destined for big things in the world of physics - how that happened I have no idea. Middle boy is going to be a ballet star or in the corp at least, and No. 1 son is one terrific musician, plays anything - and is already popular as a singer about to front his own band, when he's not studying economics. With luck he can be our auditor in years to come, keep me on the straight and narrow, haha.

It's a funny old life really. When you take stock. With luck, we have many years to come yet, hopefully together, and surely with grandchildren at some point. Although, when you say such dirty words to your kids, they all put their fingers in their ears... it's early yet of course.

I sometimes wonder how I'd have fared if my sojourn in Saughton jail had never happened at all, but I like to think I'd still have done well. It was a shame how it all went down with my parents, but I'm over all that and have been for a very long time already. I suspect we'd have fallen out big time, before much longer, although perhaps I wouldn't have been disowned. I'm convinced Mrs P had a lot to do with that, dripping poison in their ears and the lawyer they had must have thought more about his fee than advising them properly. No matter, it's not like they could have left me much of anything. Actually, they never contacted me again either, so I don't even know if they realised that the man with the same name as their erstwhile son, splashed over the hoardings around building sites all over town, was even the same man.

I had considered changing my name to that of my wife's when we married. I'm glad I didn't though, and she kept hers too. I'd rather have liked to have rubbed their noses in it, but them not wanting 'to be associated with criminals' precluded my contacting them too. I did think of turning up on their doorstep but couldn't have faced rejection so I just never risked it. How bloody sad is that? I felt sorry for my dad for a long time, but he had a tongue in his head, he could have spoken up, so I dropped that after some years.

However, I'm excited to see what the world has in store for me, for us, for our kids. There will be no disownment involved. I hope I've proved myself as a decent enough man, despite my early blips. I think it matters that people know that having been a tad wayward in youth, having been to jail even, taking 'drugs' (oh the shame!), having your parents actually officially disown you... doesn't mean you will never amount to anything. Not that everyone needs to even be as successful as I like to think I am. Just that we all deserve a chance in life, and we shouldn't assume too much about others. Or about ourselves for that matter. My *parents* went down an entirely wrong path, not me! I like to think they were just very badly advised. The Mrs. Petersons of the world should be the ones in jail maybe? Yeah, I'd vote for that!

If telling my story here helps anyone, I'm glad I've written it. We'll be away for a month or two at our place in the Dordogne in June, where the kids always join us when university breaks up, but if you feel you want to discuss more about anything I may have triggered in you, please do get in touch and I'll get back to you as soon as. My details are as below. Happy to help.

BLOOD BROTHER

BY STEVE WADE

Afraid even to get into a field with a herd of lambs. As useless as a bull with teats. And more interested in lying around in socks and turning the pages of a book than pulling on a pair of boots and getting them dirty. Those were just some of the many things Cathal's father said to and about his second-born son.

But sharper than the serrated blade of his father's buckskin hunting knife was his comment that he couldn't even get himself a girlfriend. An attack he generally made in situations and in company ripe for maximum impact.

They were having a barbecued lunch on the veranda of their renovated and modernised farmhouse. Jake, Cathal's older brother by two years, had brought home his new girlfriend for the first time. A seventeen-year-old girl of clichéd prettiness, with blonde hair and blue eyes, the boys' father was fawning over her, just as he used to with Jake's last girlfriend.

Their mom, whose onetime perfect complexion had turned to a peachy softness, was unimpressed. Cathal could see this. While she went back and forth to the kitchen to fetch the trimmings for the barbecued pheasant, her eyes she kept averted from their father.

Good old Jake, their father was saying. He had a great eye for the women. Just like his old man. This he directed at Jake's girlfriend as he forked a half a pheasant from the barbecue and laid it on the girl's plate.

"There you go," he said. "As nice a piece of cock pheasant as ever you'll get, what?"

Although he didn't want to accept it, Cathal heard the way his father deliberately alighted on the word 'cock'. And the cackle that accompanied his own stupid play on words made Cathal and Jake look at each other and shake their heads.

Later, when the boys were in the bedroom they shared, Jake would curse himself for being such an idiot to bring home a girlfriend again. Cathal could imagine it already. Jake staring hard at himself in the wardrobe mirror, his features all bunched up. Calling himself names, as though he were talking to someone else. But the language he'd use to rant about their father would be far stronger.

When the boys' mother finally sat down, their father shifted his attention and channelled all his energy into an onslaught on Cathal. As an opening statement, he said that some people might find it hard to accept that Jake and Cathal were actually brothers.

"Can you not do this, please," their mother said.

"Ah now, in fairness," their father said. "This is important." He brought to his mouth what was at least his third glass of wine and downed it in one draught.

Cathal felt his mother's hand enveloping his. For Jake's sake, he knew that she wanted to avoid a scene, as she always put it. He twisted his hand in hers so that their palms met, and their fingers entwined.

Cathal's father continued. The case he said he was putting to the ladies and gentlemen of the jury was very straightforward.

At this point, Jake tried to come to Cathal's defence by attempting to change the topic. He said that Cathal had taken some great shots on his phone of the nesting kingfisher at the bend in the river. And he'd made some great pencil sketches from the photos.

Their father slammed the table with a hammer blow of his fist.

"Jesus," their mother said.

"Respect," he said to Jake. "You may be my favourite son. But when your father speaks, by God, you'll listen to him."

Cathal watched as Jake silently debated with himself to leave the table, but remained where he was. Cathal knew his brother.

Their father squinted, turned down his mouth and nodded.

"Right," he said. "Good."

He then went on to say that anybody looking at Jake would know that he was his father. No different to looking at a prize colt in a paddock next to another with its award-winning sire. But as for the other fella, as he referred to Cathal, at which point he scrunched up his features, and pursed his lips. He left a pause, and then said there he could rest his case.

"I could," he said. "But I won't."

"Right," the boys' mother said. And before going on, apologised to Jake's girlfriend. "That's enough." She then pushed to her feet. Bad enough that her husband bullied and belittled his own son. Day and night. But to do so in front of Jake's girlfriend was nothing but cowardly.

"Cowardly?" their father said. "You're calling me a coward?"

Without responding, the boys' mother then picked up her own plate and suggested the boys and Jake's girlfriend follow her inside the house with their lunch. The boys' father needed some time alone.

Cathal took up his lunch, which he had only picked at, and followed his mother. While Jake collected his girlfriend's plate and his own. They, likewise, worked their way from the table on the veranda towards the kitchen door into the house.

Behind them came a catalogue of abuse volleyed at him by his father. Cathal cringed. Apart from bearing no resemblance to him or his brother Jake, his father shouted out that he didn't even have the bottle to take control of a quad to herd the sheep. A scaredy cat who always made sure he was sick every time there was work for real men to be done on the farm. Like repairing fences, getting a cow out of a ditch, or burning dead wood.

"Afraid he might burn his little handies," his father said. He held out a hand, palm down, and moved it in a mock tremble. And he cackled his terrible cackle.

Safe inside the house, Cathal's mother turned the key in the back door, locking it. This wasn't the first time she'd done this. It was something their father had come to expect and accept. Usually, he took himself to the lower fields. There he'd lean on a fence, smoke his pipe, and study the herd of Friesian cows. But not this time.

Outside the kitchen window, he tapped on the glass with his knuckles. Cathal had already seen him. The others turned round. Cathal dug his nails into the palm of his hand and clenched his teeth. He knew what was coming next.

"Sure, that fellah can't even pull a bird," his father said.

Cathal's mother told him not to mind what his father said. The right girl would come along for him in due course. There was no hurry. She then made a shooing gesture and sound towards the window at the man she'd married. The man who'd fathered her two boys.

Cathal glanced at Jake and flicked his eyes at Jake's girlfriend. Jake looked angry, but his girlfriend had a strange smile on her face. Laughing at him, she was, he decided. Next she was pushing herself to her feet from the wooden chair where she sat next to Jake. And Cathal watched her gliding towards him across the black and white tiles.

With no idea what she might do, Cathal's senses were paralysed. That's when he felt the blue-eyed, blonde girl's soft lips pressed against his cheek.

"You're so cute," she said, and she ran the side of her finger across the corner of his eye. And then, unbelievably, she put her arms about his neck and drew him to her and held him tighter than Jake did when he pretended to be a wrestler. And she told him not to cry. But, whereas Jake sometimes left him feeling suffocated and dazed, Jake's girlfriend made him feel warm and fuzzy inside. This was the first time a girl had ever kissed him or hugged him.

Unable to stop himself from really crying now, Cathal pulled away from her. He then ran from the kitchen and pounded up the stairs to his and Jake's bedroom. This time, instead of his father's cackling, it was Jake's nervous high-pitched laugh that followed him. The laugh he reserved for embarrassment or guilt.

Later that night, just as Cathal knew he would, Jake banged on about what a gobshite he was for letting his girlfriend see the madhouse he lived in. But he acted even crazier than Cathal had expected him to do. Besides referring to their father as pig-dad - the name he used when he was especially pissed-off with their father – he slammed his palm against his own forehead several times.

Not until Jake was at last snoring, and mumbling in his sleep, did Cathal finally have room in his head to toy with some ideas that had earlier awoken during his father's tirade of abuse. These ideas he worked on and reshaped the way he executed his pencil sketches. He examined his subject from all angles. He scrutinised the details, considered depth, perspective, light and shade, until he had a clear understanding of the overall picture of what it meant and what he was after and how he might achieve those effects and outcome.

By Friday morning, Cathal had the perfect opportunity to put into motion the first of his plans. He knew that Jake had already told his girlfriend he wouldn't see her till Sunday. He had rugby practice, and then the trip to the Aviva Stadium on Saturday to watch the Six Nations final with his club. And they were staying in Dublin overnight.

When Jake asked Cathal if he'd seen his Smartphone, Cathal, naturally, didn't tell him he had taken it, put it on silent, and hidden it where nobody would ever think of looking. Instead, he made a few suggestions as to where Jake might have left it. But, unable to find it, Cathal allowed his brother to use his phone and let his girlfriend know she could contact him on Cathal's number until Friday afternoon. Cathal would pass on the messages. And, until he left for Dublin, let him use his phone too.

But, as soon as Jake had left for the bus with his club, Cathal, masquerading as his big brother, sent Jake's girlfriend a text telling her the trip to Dublin was off and could they meet up that evening.

As arranged, Jake's girlfriend was waiting outside the old cinema in town at five.

"Cathal?" she said when she saw him crossing the road from the fast-food joint where he'd been watching and waiting. "What are you doing here?"

But, before he could answer, she'd given him a kiss like the one she'd planted on his cheek a few days ago. So, his instincts were right. She was obviously confused about her interest in Jake. Why else would she kiss him? And especially now when Jake wasn't around?

Cathal explained to her that Jake had come down with something. That he couldn't make it but had already booked the seats for the movie.

"He said for me to come in his place." In his own voice he heard a tremble as he said this. He let his eyes slide down her yellow top to her black leggings. This made him tremble more.

Suddenly Jake's girlfriend looked worried. Or confused. She bit her lip and said maybe she should call him. Cathal hadn't figured this into his plan. But, luckily, her eyes widened, and she said she was stupid. Jake didn't have his phone anyway.

Before she remembered that people - parents and stuff - also had land lines, Cathal said the movie was about to start, and did she want popcorn or something?

The movie Cathal had chosen was a gory one about a hunter who gets injured while hunting and is abandoned to die by his fellow hunters. Cathal had already seen it with Jake. Something told him Jake's girl-friend would react just the way he'd seen girls behave with their boyfriends when he saw it the first time.

"Oh my God," she said. "I can't watch this." She turned her head away from the screen and away from Cathal. When it was safe to look, Cathal patted the back of her hand.

She reacted in the same way to the next disturbing scene, only this time she turned her head Cathal's way and buried her face into his shoulder. Cathal grasped her hand the way his mom grasped his. And, incredibly, she accepted it and squeezed hard.

By the end of the movie, Cathal was experiencing excruciating pain below his stomach between his legs. He wished he'd worn his tracksuit bottoms instead of his tight jeans. This pain dissipated somewhat when he was walking Jake's girlfriend home along the towpath by the canal.

Laughing nervously about Cathal's choice of movie, she said she wished she could unsee what she'd seen. And how she hoped she'd never have to watch a movie like that one anytime for the rest of her life. She then start talking about how pretty the white blossoms on the trees were. She pointed to a long-legged bird plopping into the water. Its legs olive-green. Cathal told her it was a coot.

When Cathal moved in close enough so that he could feel her body heat, she skipped on ahead of him, her ass wiggling invitingly. She was teasing him. But he didn't have time for games. They were already nearing the bank that led up to the stretch that would lead them to her house. He'd been waiting for the moment, the signal to let him know she wanted him to make his move.

He turned his neck and looked over his shoulder. Nobody. And neither was there anybody ahead of them. Apart from a man walking his dog on the other side of the bank going in the other direction, it was just the two of them, the cherry blossoms, and the trilling of the birds in the trees.

Cathal felt himself taking a few quick steps after her and slapping her on the ass.

"Ow. Cathal, that hurt." She rubbed her hand where he'd slapped her. Her face looked deadly serious.

Not the reaction he'd expected. Not the way he'd ever seen her react to Jake when he slapped her. He slapped her again and laughed. But his own laugh sounded more vicious than upbeat.

"Stop. Stop it." She began to break into a fast walk, which quickly became a fast run.

Cathal took off after her and felt himself diving on her the way Jake often rugby-tackled him. Her momentum and his brought her to the ground, with Cathal atop her. Which, in turn, sent the pair of them tumbling and sliding down the embankment to the water's edge. She screamed and he laughed a snarly laugh.

A raft of mallard drakes, intent on subduing a hen, took off from the water, their deep and echoless quacks a wild and cranky complaint on being disturbed.

"No," she said. Please, don't. What're you doing? Let me up. I'm wet."

"Well, let's get these things off you so," he said, and yanked hard, first at her yellow top, which ripped, leaving one of her white breasts exposed. This fleshy mound Cathal grabbed, which sent electricity shooting to his head.

"Get off me," she said, and he felt her nails raking the back of his hand, the instant stinging pain somehow feeding his frenzy of desire.

"You cut me," he said, and twisted and raised his hand so that he smeared her white cheek in red.

"Help," she screamed. "Help me."

Cathal clamped his injured hand over her mouth, while she twisted and squirmed. Her eyes as wild and petrified as a spooked horse.

"Stay down," he said, and used strength he never knew he had to push her farther into the reeds. Ignoring the slashing nails that were lashing out and connecting with his face and neck, Cathal used his other hand to tear and pull at her leggings from the waist. She fought hard to twist free, but he succeeded in getting the leggings down below her knees. He then fumbled with the belt of his own jeans and, like something he had seen often on porn sites, he was inside her.

"No," she managed to squeeze out through the palm he pressed over her mouth. And she closed tight her eyes, and turned her head to face the canal waters.

"Look at me," he said. He twisted her head so that her eyes met his before she again squeezed them shut.

And he felt himself thrusting hard, as though it were something he'd done a thousand times. To the rhythm of his own grunts, he moved on her and in her. The white fire in his loins a confusion of pain and pleasure. Beneath him, Jake's girlfriend no longer resisted. But neither did she move with him. She lay there, her clothes now soaked through from the squelchy reed-bed, resigned to Cathal's thrusts. The contorted expression on her face that of someone witness to something so repulsive she would accept death as an option if it were presented to her..

The inside of Cathal's head burned hotly. With his hands now wrapped about her neck, he slammed into her harder and quicker.

Her eyes blinked open. Gone the blue-eyed prettiness. In its place her true ugliness, which, in turn, was mirrored in her contorted features. The kind of face that Cathal despised. A face the world could do without. A face he would annihilate. And he would have too, had not his hands slackened and grown limp following the final thrust of his loins.

Conscious only then of Jake's girlfriend's gasping for breath, he rolled off her. All the anger, the untamed desire, the impulse that almost pushed him to do the unthinkable spent. Used up.

The sound of her convulsive crying raked behind his eyes. And the sight of her fumbling to pull up her drenched leggings the most pathetic thing he'd ever seen.

Unable to look into her face, Cathal held out his hand to her as she scrambled up the bank.   But she sidled from him, pushed herself upright, and took off in the direction of her street.

About his stomach, Cathal felt the grasp of an invisible hand. It squeezed. Into his mouth came the bitter aftertaste of ice cream and popcorn from the cinema. When purged and rested, he, likewise, took off for his house. A place he knew he would never again call home.

Back in his house that evening, Cathal awaited and expected the police to call at any moment. Or maybe the girl's father. And her brothers and uncle.

He couldn't eat. He watched the clock, checked his phone, and imagined himself holed up in his room, his father's semi-automatic rifle resting on his lap. Loaded. His eyes on the doorhandle. Alternatively, he saw himself rushing across the fields by moonlight. Behind him loud men with barking dogs. Like in the movies.

By bedtime, nobody had come to take him away. Not even a phone call to his parents, letting them know what he had done. Perhaps she hadn't told anyone. Could be that maybe she'd secretly enjoyed it after all.

Lying awake in his and Jake's bedroom without Jake in the upper bunk, a smile broke across Cathal's face. He saw himself approach his father and ask him, now who couldn't pull a bird? But this was something he knew he would never do. And the more he tried to fool himself that he would, the greater his resentment grew towards his father. And with this resentment, returned the uncontrollable rage he had earlier felt when on the canal bank with Jake's girlfriend. Driven by this feeling, he eased himself from bed, left his room and worked his way downstairs and out into the garage. The time had arrived to put into action the second part of his plan.

Not too long after this, flashing lights reflect and glisten in the puddles on the winding driveway leading up to the farmhouse. The whine of police and fire brigade sirens. Authoritative, uniformed male voices usher the gathering neighbours in pyjamas and dressing gowns to move back. Cathal's mother and father, and men, women and children, with eyes widened in shock, fascination, and terror. A few afire with pleasure. The firemen in yellow coats manipulating the water mains, their tools clanking and clanging as they attach hoses in vain attempts to extinguish the flames that consume the rebuilt farmhouse. The house Cathal has grown up in for the last sixteen years.

On his face, Cathal feels the stinging heat that comes off the uncontrollable inferno. Inside him there rages another type of fire as he listens to the cracking and splitting of timber, as he watches beams fall and crash. In their wake - lava explosions. And in his nostrils, the wind-shifted smells of burning wood and the fishy odour of melting plastic mingles with the acrid stench of burning electricity wires.

Cathal's entire being, like the blaze, is afire with a sense of power, of unstoppable invincibility. A house and home that had sheltered two generations. That watched as new infants arrived and grew into adulthood. A fortress that witnessed countless family sagas and kept the tales. All annihilated at the single stroke of a match. Well, three strokes. The match Cathal struck on the striking surface didn't ignite until the third stroke.

In Cathal's head, aflame in bold red capitals, his father's words:

CAN'T EVEN GET HIMSELF A GIRLFRIEND.

AFRAID HE MIGHT BURN HIS LITTLE HANDIES.

THE DEVIL'S RESTING PLACE

BY LUKE VARNEY

CHAPTER 1 - THE DEVIL'S RESTING PLACE

FOR WHY DO YOU WEAR THAT HOOD, OLD ONE? IS IT TO COVER UP those scars? A young child asks her Elder. In a small Icelandic town the wind blows strong and the ice chills bones. Akureyri is its name, and the snow is just as cold as this old killer's heart. The shores as black as the Devil's soul, in search for that sacred fire in a field of ice and bones. For this hooded figure shall hunt the Devil's resting place and pierce his soul with the bone of an innocent. Take this bitter drink, child, and you too shall join me in the hunt for the Devil's resting place. Yours will be in spirit and mine in person, be them the same thing I do not know.

For Hellbound I am child, for my past and future sins. Drink this bitter drink child, imagine a brighter future where we shall meet at the Devil's resting place. The hooded figure then handed the girl the drink of hemlock. He knew deep within his soul that an innocent life must be taken to reach that ice-laden tomb. For the Devil took his son in a battle of stormy seas long ago. If damnation be his fate, then so it be, he shall become the Devil to save his offspring from an eternal icy grave.

We are outlaws and adventurers in this small Icelandic town and so our family blood has been stained from child to child. What will one more innocent life taken matter to our veins of corrupted kinship? Child, I must ask you, leave this crooked shack and look across our distant arctic harbour. The frosty air will allow you to see the sun in a whole new light. Child, ensure you take that bitter drink with you. Its bitterness is mystical and will turn our snow-covered sea into a new realm of possibility.

Walking out of the shack and towards the harbour, the child took a small sip of the bitter drink. Although bitter, it didn't taste all that bad. She believed the man's honey-dewed words and desperately wanted to leave this land of ice and pain. This potion will take her toward a new land of magic and scripture. She knew it deep in her very heart. Looking towards that frosted old sun, she took a deep breath and a shallow gulp. The sun had begun to set as her belly grew warmer. The stars slowly coming out of their long-awaited hiding, so distant and out of reach.

Extending out her arm to grab a star, she could feel her heart melt. Slowly, this warm sensation began spreading across her whole body. For she had become the sun, the stars, and the moon all encompassed into one. Her legs became as weak as jelly, causing her to fall backwards.

The bitter drink had reached its intoxicating peak as she lay on her back, paralyzed. Twilight formed into a duality of light and darkness. The stars and the sun existing in one photographic entity. This theatrical dance of dimming stars had the agonising brightness of the setting sun behind it. She innocently gazed at that setting sun, and in a way, it reminded her of herself. The brightness in her belly, so warm and comforting as her eyes closed. Finally, she could rest.

Darkness encompassed her very soul. Her final thoughts were of the hooded figure and how he had made her life finally complete.

Far away from the drama being played out on the harbour, the hooded figure watched the tormented play take place. For the first time in his sinful life, he felt a shimmer of regret.

Although his mission of sin and glory remained firmly in place. His heart pounded at the chance to redeem his son's life, finally adding another sequence to arriving at the Devil's resting place. In the commotion of adrenaline, the hooded figure grabbed a nearby rock and ran towards the girl's freshly made corpse. Smashing it onto her leg with ritualistic precision. Just above the knee, as the ancient

texts foretold. Using all the force in his body, he plunged the rock onto her rigid corpse. Continuing until he heard a loud crunching noise. With surgical precision, he then removed a section of her femur. With the bone of an innocent simply being a sinful stepping stone in his dreaded mission. Placing the stone gently back on the ground, he wiped his eyes with his sleeve, allowing a long-awaited sense of relief to overtake his body. By tooth or nail, he will complete his ill-fated mission. For he knows he shall see that girl again at the sacred mound of fire and ice. He knows by the blackness of his beating heart that this is the story to end all stories: the story to engulf this realm in eternal darkness.

CHAPTER 2 - THE CREATURE IN THE CAVE

Miles away from that crooked old shack, a creature of twisted fate lurks in a morbid cave. Its mind warped by the eternal Icelandic moonshine. This is a creature formed by darkness and winter snow. A creature hunted and demonised by the townsfolk below. Within this town, a hunter receives a contract to be paid in gold. Obliging him to capture this lonesome creature and send it far away from this shivering land. The townsfolk gift a burning torch and a piercing dagger to help illuminate any path before the Hunter. With his quest given, the hunter stumbles into the dead night of winter. Ready to wage war against this creature and damn his fate away from this land.

Marching through the snow, the hunter felt a strange sense of unease. Whispering voices scratched at his mind, pleading for him to turn around and return to his comfortable village life. However, it was far too late for cowardice. His fate had already been bound. After a steep climb through miles of snow, he arrived at the cave. Observing an extensive collection of hanging moss blocking its entrance. Walking slowly towards the gloomy cave. He gently placed his burning torch upon its mouldy blockage, causing a plume of smoke to enrich the moonlit air. The slow burn of the fire contrasted deeply with the snow-covered mountainous hills.

As he crouched through the burning embers, a chill passed through his quivering core. There was certainly no turning back now. All that lay before him was the slow descending crawl through the darkness ahead of him. The only thought he could muster at such a moment was a burning hatred toward this forsaken creature. In his mind's eye, the burrowing crawl seemed to last for an eternity. Unaided by the fact he could barely see an inch in front of his face. The flame of his torch being an uncomfortably weak ally at such a moment. After an eternity of arduous crawling, the landscape of the cave gradually changed, and signs of life finally emerged.

The dampness of the cave, replaced by dry wooden flooring and the damp glow of a nearby lantern.

Clearly, this damned creature was nearby and thriving. A break was met from his seemingly endless crawling, with his knee buckling against something hard and metal. A lonesome hatchway laid out by the creature to exit during foraging. As he placed his trembling hand upon the cold metal handle, a clockwise turn caused a subtle clicking sound to be produced. Tumbling towards his long-awaited destiny as the hatch suddenly swung open. Finding the tormented creature feeding off the flesh of a recently harvested raven. With stealth in mind, he cast his torch behind his back. Hoping to avoid the creature's peripheral vision as he slowly crawled toward it. Unbeknownst to the Hunter, bad luck had reared its ugly head. The torch had settled on dry hay, causing a whimpering flame to transform into a roaring blaze.

The flame caused our creature of the cave to be blinded with painful sensitivity. For you are barely human, aren't you? That trauma and isolation has made your skin as pale as moonlight. For it is the creatures of the night that thrive in the darkness, their bones as twisted as their minds. But when the sun rises and your soul becomes as red as hot coals, then you shall transform. Not of this creature dwelling in this swelling cave, but a part of society once again.

Your hair shall grow back and your skin will represent a glowing of health, just as it has before. Welcomed back to the clan in your hour of torment. Their open arms will feel just as warm as the sun's rays. We have missed you, as that creature was just in your imagination. For we all become that creature in that cave from time to time.

CHAPTER 3 - THE BRANDING OF A CREATURE

The creature's initial reaction was to snarl and growl at such a honey-dewed statement. For it knew the hatred held by the townsfolk below all too well. The few words it remembered came out broken and feral. Losing its humanity for so long had taken a toll. A question lingered in the hunter's mind. Did it even still see itself as human? The townsfolk certainly didn't see it that way, and so it neglected all pleasantries, even to itself. The creature in the cave was all it knew, all it had known for so long. For even when it was a person, the branding of an outcast screamed unhuman and so this label became its social and psychological branding.

The branding: so painful and scolding that it became part of its very soul. Leaving no other option than to become a creature of the cave. The minds of others had forced its fate towards that of a dehumanised existence. Our gold-hearted hero let his moral purity guide his actions, offering his hand to console the beast. Expecting the creature to take his hand with a calm embrace and a hearty grasp. However, the creature had a different plan in mind. Letting out a cough of raven feathers and a shrill scream of "No!". The creature extended its mouth and, with one fluid motion, latched onto our hero's hand. Flailing and screaming to remove the creature in desperation, a crunch of bone could be heard echoing across the cave. For when you brand a human, a creature, a creature is all it shall remain.

The hunter let out a blood-curdling scream as his bones crunched. Thrusting his thumb into the beast's eye, he desperately tried to escape. He had offered all of his humanity to this lonesome creature, only to receive a defiant refusal in return. Reaching for his weapon, he plunged it into the beast's neck. Repeatedly stabbing the creature. The beast replied with a long-awaited whimpered cry. Its pain transferred into a feral rage, desperately trying to bite off the hero's hand. Stabbing the beast multiple times was the only way to free his bloody hand. After the painstaking struggle was over, the beast lay dead in a bloody puddle of its own making. Our hero could only stare blankly at the stump where his hand used to be. His hand lay twitching on the floor and his face turned a shade of pale moonlight. Replying to the pathetic scene that had taken place. The hunter kicked the creature's ribs, causing them to break.

The hunter watched the creature's rib cage pant as its mouth overflowed with blood. All he could think about at such a moment was the similarities between the body of the beast and a freshly slain animal. The creature let out its final gargled words "Father, I'm coming home." Causing the hunted to shed a single tear. The hunter could only feel sympathy for the creature. Its soul used to be human, after all, and so did its flesh.

With its soul leaving its body, the little humanity it had left was restored. A long-awaited end to a pitiful existence.

CHAPTER 4 - A RETURN TO SIN

Returning once again to that icy harbour, the hooded figure had just wiped the last of his tears from his frosty cheeks. The eye-stinging play he had just directed had just come to a pitiful end. It was now time to play his final role. Walking slowly towards that harbour of desecration, he gave the girl only a passing glance. His sight transfixed solely upon his future, ignoring the depression of his past. As he placed his withered bones into a snow-covered rowboat. He began his laboured journey northwards, deep into the distant arctic wasteland. His bones crunched and cracked with each stroke of the oars. He had vowed this sequence would take place years before. A last act of synchronicity with his long-departed son, fulfilling the pact to join him in the burrows of icy water and bone-aching cold.

Memories of that night so long ago haunted his twisted mind. In darkness, they came through stormy black seas to raid their heart's desires and claim what they did not own. Raiders from Norway, attempting to find a fortune after their murderous exile months before. Bloodthirst was in their eyes, their very blood pumping to savage their prey and conquer this untouched land. His hand placed upon the shoulder of his courageous son, with the stormy black skies igniting the sea below. A field of lightning sparked the waves below as the sea grew taller and taller.

Nature's mission of moral purity opposed the banished Scandinavian explorers. It was almost as if the Gods themselves were trying to expel the unwanted conquerors back to the land from which they came.

That night of adrenaline and bloodthirst. That night when the villagers feared their inhuman raiders, through sword and torch they took what was unrightfully theirs. A father's love for his child, so simple and true. So proud of his blood-curdling scream into the darkness of battle. When the pinnacle of war arrived, courage and rage were needed most. A godsend of a wave took the hooded figure's son and dragged him into the depths below that fateful night. In grief, he searched the aftermath of those scorched waters for weeks upon end. The only remnants of that frightful night being a sword he had given his child as a boy, burrowed deep beneath black sands.

The hooded figure, to the detriment of his soul, witnessed that event. His only son dragged to the depths of that frosted sea. His offspring, the only thing in this cursed world that he truly loved. Dragged into the depths of a frozen hell. Cursing the Devil for the whispered instructions he gave his spawn. For when you take away a man's capacity to love, a beast is all he can become. After all, the easiest way into damnation is a willing partitioning of one's soul.

This is the painful story he will tell himself for years to come, becoming the very thing he cursed that morbid night.

The titanic wave that thrashed his son into its icy depths was nature's way of ensuring protection to the victims of this brigade of sword and fire. Death flashed before the boy's eyes as he sunk into the depths below. With a gasp of air, he awoke upon that black tormented beach. The battle was over and the village had found a new creature to scapegoat. The source of their pain was to be hung and quartered in front of a roaring crowd. Tied up and captured in simple fishing nets, the villagers dragged him squirming into the town hall.

Many thought of hanging him for his crimes against their innocent and weak. A fitting end for an outlaw and a criminal. However, a single voice of reason stopped their screaming barbarism. A blonde-haired girl with more compassion than all the village combined. Pleading the villagers from atop the hanging station, she shouted and begged. Proposing that the boy should be exiled to a place where he won't hurt anyone ever again. A lonesome cave in the mountains. A place where he shall contemplate his actions and misdeeds. He shall repent for his sins and return a free man for the village to embrace. Or he shall bathe in his painful sins and transform slowly into an isolated beast, imprisoned within a lofty mountain. One day they shall send her older brother to drag him from the depths of agonising reflection. A final chance to repent and become human once again.

On that pivotal day, that little girl set the fate of many in stone. Alas, the hooded figure still took that blonde-haired girl's life years later. Oblivious to the transaction that had taken place between her and his son. The bitter-sweet truth being that his son could have been saved that night so long ago. If only the courage of heart was present to reconcile his long-lasting feud. In his mind, he shall forever relive that night of stormy seas. The only peace of mind coming from the day he meets his rest. For he still seeks the Devil's resting place.

CHAPTER 5 - A PALE BODY FOR A PALE SEA

The wind blows strong in the waters outside of that small Icelandic town. Akureyri is its name and the snow is just as cold as this old killer's heart. Drifting northwards away from that harbour of desecration, our killer removed his black hood. His face was sombre as he provided a ritualistic kiss to his dagger of bone. A final goodbye to the girl he had savaged days before.

The ritualistic ceremony continued as he casually attached a noose around his neck. Connecting the other side of the neck-snapping rope to a large rock he had collected previously at the harbour. Without hesitation, he relinquished the rock into the icy waters. Watching the rope slowly unravel as his neck jolted sharply. His pale body dragged into the depths below. The final sequence of his long-awaited mission. To die as his son had, dragged to the bottom of the frozen ocean to meet the Devil himself. A submerged sacrifice of his black beating soul. As the icy water encompassed his pale body, his eyes froze from the hypothermic shock. A draugr of old, deep inside an ancient arctic tomb.

The Devil only knows how long his corpse lay within those black sands. Time warped itself around his corpse. A second felt like a year and a year felt like an eon. To his surprise, he desperately gasped for air as he awoke. Coughing up the entire ocean, he tried to regain the life in his pale, dead eyes. His instincts kicked in after his spluttered recovery, wielding his dagger of bone in hand. His veins aching to inflict the pain of his miserable life on the dark one himself. He had envisioned this moment for so long. His blurred vision allowed him to catch a brief glimpse of the figure in front of him. Frantically, he flailed towards the figure in a stabbing motion. The distinct sound of his knife perforating the figure's chest echoed across the chamber. As the warm blood began pooling around his hand, the hooded figure slowly came to his senses.

As his vision cleared, he knew that his dreaded mission was finally over. After years of torment, his long-awaited rest was near. The mortally wounded figure fell to his knees, his soul separating from his core. However, to his detriment, he had not pierced the soul of the Devil.

Instead, he had plunged his knife into the chest of his son. His son crouched onto his knees, staring at the imprint of bone buried deep within his chest. Pure horror encompassed both of their souls. Every waking moment had led the hooded figure toward his twisted fate. For he took the life of an innocent at that frozen harbour, and a manifestation of karma had bitten back twice as hard. The tragedy being that his love for his son turned into the cold, dismayed emptiness of death. Dropping to his knees in torment, he knew a cruel trick had been placed upon him. His life of cruelty and sin transferred into the shattering of his son's soul. An icy hand reached up from behind the hooded figure, placing itself upon his shaking shoulder.

As the hand comforted the hooded figure, he watched the only person he had ever loved shrivel away into the void. As he turned to face the owner of that comforting hand, a part of him knew who it would be. He knew her all too well. It was the innocent one, the betrayed, the defiled. The girl in the shack who once respected him. Her soul had dissolved into ether, just like his son had moments before. Her words were just as innocent and honeyed as when he had first met her.

Whispering in the hooded figure's ear, she told him of her life before. Of how she saved his son from the hanging station in the raided village. Telling him that her thoughts, just before death, were of purity and faith. Sometimes it's easier to break someone with kindness than it is with simple spite. She still looked up to him in a way. Her life was simple here. For she exists as the daughter of Hel and her life is uplifted by her cold love.

Looking into the eyes of the man, she could see how broken he had become. His eyes were so frightening in the cold, for we now know what lurks below. Deep inside that eye, we enter the memories of a past time ago. A knife in the tear-laced shimmer, a dance to make us all shudder. You remember that event, don't you? The knife to your soul, the hood to cover up your traumatic forebode. When your offspring was desecrated at sea, a drowning flame to ignite his pin-pricked soul forever. Remember that I'm here for you until those memories fade, until our bones cross in a steeple's deep hole. When the passage of time heals like an imprint of gold onto your timeless woes. For we shall see the afterlife as the defence to life's unforgiving blows. Whispered the girl to the hooded figure.

Emerging from that ritual site of ice and bone, a goddess of the dead and long-lost souls arrived. Her body split between the living and the dead. Rotten flesh on one side of her face and mortal cold eyes on the other. For the Devil did not truly rest here. The real strings pulling this man's puppeteered limbs was Hel. Alongside her, as it had always been, was her daughter she had sent into the mortal world long ago. Both of their icy hands lifted the hooded figure back onto his feet. They forgave him for what he had done. Time shall be the only judge of his corrupted soul. Allowing him to continue walking towards his fate, laid out so long ago. For Helheim will never open its doors to him, his soul shall be bound elsewhere.

CHAPTER 6 - A MEETING WITH THE HANGED

Pity was all Hel and her daughter could feel at such a moment. After all, their plan had worked to perfection. Hel's hands placed their grip on reality's strings well before the boy's arrival on Iceland's black shores.

With the rot of isolation, a creature is all he could have become. Hel then placed her next chess piece. Allowing our hero to approach that lonesome cave. His life was to be sacrificed for the greater good of the universe, dying from blood loss within that lonesome cave. Our hero was a proud son of Hel. A title held deep within his soul. The sacrificial lamb to be slaughtered and returned to the kingdom of his mother's bosom. A hero heralded amongst the dead and forgotten souls of Helheim. The girl and her brother shall thus rule this realm as gods, with their mother's icy hands guiding their every move.

The one-eyed god made a deal with Hel so long ago. Sealing the hooded figure's fate far away from Hel's domain. His soul to be bound within the realm of the all-father. As a black pool of water emerged beneath his feet, the room fell deathly silent. He knew this was the end of his life and, like a defeated dog, he accepted his fate with his tail beneath his legs. As he gave one last glance at the girl, his eyes were full of regret. All the girl could do was smile at such a moment.

Despite all that he did to her, she still loved him as a Father figure and forgave him for his misdeeds. As the hooded figure placed his exhausted limbs into the rising black pool, two hands of tar took hold of him, dragging him into the realm of the all-father.

In the void, far away from where our eyes can see. Lies a tree made of tears, its sap as black as black can be. Sorrow and pain compressed into ink that burrows into its rooted debris. An ominous galaxy can be seen watching that black tree. Gazing at its agonising limbs for so crooked are thee. As the hooded figure approaches, he looks upon its twisted limbs, disturbed by what he can see. His eyes are met with black tear drops as he looks up to that weeping old tree. Reality dissolves, leaving him knowing that nothing is all there can be.

As he awakes, he is entwined in vine. Captured within the damp embrace of that crooked old tree. That tree that lay weeping, waiting for another lifeless soul to complete thee. His story is as old as life can be. For his capture within that weeping old tree releases the darkness bestowed upon thee. As his eyes darted toward the opposing branch of the tree, he noticed a lifeless body swinging in the void. A man wearing a frayed black cloak and a long flowing beard. Upon looking at this corpse, its eyes rapidly opened. Revealing the stark difference between the white health of his left eye and the black hole encapsulating his right. In response to the old man's awakening, the tree tightened its grip.

"You cannot stop the narrative of your own creation. Your eyes shall never see flowers bloom, you shall never hear a child's laugh. You have damned humanity with your selfish actions.

Without the sun, darkness shall take hold of the earth. I put you on your journey of pain, knowing full well what morbid choices you shall take. You are rotten to the core, and worst of all, you do not care." With a brief gasp of air, the old man grew silent. Only for his rant to begin again with increased rage and intensity. "For I am Odin! The hanged god! The all-father of humanity! You shall remain here for all of eternity. The choices made were not mine, after all.

This is a fate of your own choosing." With these binding words, Odin damned the hooded figure to remember his miserable life for all of eternity within the damp embrace of the crooked tree.

His soul slowly dripped into the collection of ink beneath his feet, providing tortured memories for the ink pool to replay. Meanwhile, the girl shall live a glorious life with her family in Helheim. Thinking of the hooded figure only in passing, just as he did with her corpse eons ago.

The eternal Icelandic moonshine turned black, spreading across the planet like a plague of black ink. Infecting the sun until it turned into a dark shade of ink.

The hooded figure could only innocently gaze at that blackening sun. In a way, it reminded him of himself. The darkness in his soul, so warm and comforting, now fading into an eternal darkness. His last thought was of that innocent girl, of how she had smiled at him before his eternal torment. All he knows now is all he ever knew: the path to that sacred tomb of fire and ice is forsaken, and he shall become the place that only existed in his twisted imagination. For he had finally become the Devil's resting place.

THE INCIDENT AT SEA

BY KATE WRITER

It had taken the tailors in Hanoi two days to make my brother Tyrone's magic cloak because of all the anime characters he wanted hand sewn onto the material in red and white. He looked like Dracula in it. One of the boat's crew passed by and glanced at him. Tyrone did a big, majestic wave, and pulled the edges of the cloak up to his eyes. He fixed the man with his dead stare, the one he thought gave him power over people. I shivered in the cold and told him I was going back to our cabin.

The boat was in Halong Bay, one of the top ten tourist wonders of the world. I had never heard of it before this holiday in Vietnam. We were with Mrs Harris and her daughter Zoe who went to my school. They had been going on the holiday with another family who had had to cancel. When she heard this, Mum straightaway, without asking us, told her we'd love to go. The timing suited her, she said. But I knew it was because she was mad at our father. She left it till the last minute to let him know.

We had more luggage than we were meant to bring. As we'd clambered off the small ferry onto the boat for our overnight stay at Halong Bay the crew – who were all small slim Vietnamese guys - hung back, in no mood to hoist it up on board. We could've left it at the hotel, and with the minibus driver who had offered to mind it, but Mum hadn't trusted it not to go missing.

Mum said, 'Terrible service,' in the direction of another family. The mother wore a thin gold and red sari-style dress that reached her ankles. She was shivering despite wearing a puffer jacket.The father told us his name was Sanjay. He did all the talking while his two kids, aged about 10 and twelve, just stared silently at us.

Two other people crossed the ramp after us: a big man with heavy black eyebrows and jowly chin who when Mum asked, said he was a professor of art from Croatia. His girlfriend looked like she could have been one of his students. She said she was from Brazil. She had long black wavy hair. He was holding her hand but I saw him look at Zoe. A slow gaze. Up and down.

Our guide, a short Vietnamese man in a grubby grey puffer jacket, began to hand out the cabin keys. Tyrone and I went to our room so Tyrone could organise his gear. He could take hours.

We gathered later in the main cabin to meet up with the guide. He spoke softly and his English was too hard to follow, so I switched off.

'Daniel, did you follow that?' Mum prodded me with her elbow.

'No, what?'

'He says there's a storm coming, and they might have to cancel the trip.'

'When? Right now?' I thought about it. I wouldn't have minded seeing inside the famous limestone caves but it was freezing out here on the boat. We could go back to shore and stay at one of the big hotels by the harbour. They'd have internet and cable TV and we wouldn't be stuck out here in these choppy waves.

'No,' the man said, turning to me like I was in charge. He spoke more slowly now, stressing the words more. 'No. We will still go. But we will see only the one cave.' He looked at me, waiting for a response. 'And we're going to overnight in a different bay,' he said. 'In the China sea.' He paused: 'China less restrictions. It's okay for us.'

'Okay,' I said.

But Mum didn't take it so well. 'What's this?' She raised her voice deliberately to get everyone else's attention. 'It's not good enough.'

Sanjay turned towards her. His wife looked up at him in alarm.

The professor reached out to take his girlfriend's hand. He had beefy hands with black hairs all over the backs of them; hers were tiny and pale and hairless.

'Did you hear what the guide said?' Mum said loudly. 'It's not good enough. They would've known about the weather before we got on. I'm going to phone the travel agent in Hanoi, tell them what I think of this.'

This was the kind of thing Mum did all the time since she and Dad broke up. It was like she was always anticipating people would take advantage of her. So, she'd be nasty before they could.

The guide looked down. He said nothing.

Zoe glared at me. It wasn't fair. It was nothing to do with me. I stood up and went over to the windows. Outside, the sea was grey, the sky a matching pewter with drizzle coming down from it.

When I turned back the professor had begun smooching with his girlfriend. I wanted to call out, Get a room, old man.

Tyrone went out onto the deck. I could see him doing his big evil, *Look at me, I have powers.*

There's nothing I can do to stop Tyrone being weird. It's like I couldn't stop my older brother, Jake, pushing me under the strong waves at the beach when I was ten. He held me down and I couldn't move. When he let me go, my feet couldn't touch the sea bed. I panicked and flailed around until an old Māori man who'd been playing at the water's edge with his grandchild swam out and pulled me from the water.

Afterwards, when I told Mum – who'd been reading on the beach – that Jake had tried to drown me, she dismissed the whole thing. 'Oh, Daniel,' she said. 'You're exaggerating. It wasn't like that at all. Jake was just playing.' It was after this I first began to stutter even though Mum says it was much later. She says she remembers when exactly.

To get to see the world-famous cave we had to travel once more on a smaller ferry boat. The professor was the first to step onto it. But then he flailed about and had to grasp the side of a bench seat to stop himself falling onto the deck. When he caught me laughing, he scowled.

The little ferry splashed around a lot, flimsy in the rough sea. I began to feel seasick. I wished I were back on the shore. Long after my near drowning, the one Mum said didn't happen, she had made me take lessons with Tyrone in the school's outdoor pool. She said she didn't like him doing things on his own. The pool was always cold when you got in and never really heated up but I got used to it. Being in the open sea here, though, was making me feel uneasy.

Up front the professor lurched up from his wooden seat, preparing to take pictures of the line of limestone islands that could be seen through the mist at the end of the bay.

He fumbled with his camera, stumbling a little. From behind us, the Vietnamese captain, shouted, 'Hey, you. Sit.'

The professor stayed standing.

The captain shouted something angrily in Vietnamese. The puffer jacket man began to make his way down the middle aisle between the seats.

Behind me, Mum was saying to Mrs Harris: 'I made sure there's nothing of my ex in the new house, he's such a loser.'

I turned around to shush her but she didn't take any notice. 'And would you believe he thinks phoning the kids a couple of times a month is being a father? God, he's such a plonker–'

The guide had reached the professor. He pointed to a sign, showing an outline of a standing figure with a red cross through it. He said something quietly so no one would've heard him, but it was still enough to get the professor riled.

'Listen here.' The professor had a deep growling voice.

The guide said, 'It is dangerous. You will fall overboard.'

'For God's sake, man, I am not a child,' the professor shouted back. 'I can bloody swim.' He remained on his feet.

Now it was the captain's turn to shout even louder.

'Sit down, sir, please.' The guide spoke in an urgent tone. But still polite.

The professor's face darkened. 'You hear me? I do what I want.'

The guide held out his arm towards the other's elbow. As if this small insignificant man in his roly poly puffer jacket could possibly hope to pull such a heavy ox back into sitting position.

Then it was the girlfriend's turn. She pulled at her boyfriend's jacket.

He sat down then, with a show of reluctance. 'What does he think I am? A baby?' He flicked his fingers petulantly.

The girlfriend leaned over and kissed him which shut him up. They tongue kissed. Yuk. Gross. I looked away. Zoe glared at me, I wasn't sure why. Maybe she thought I was enjoying watching them.

We arrived at the dock and the guide led us in single file up steps to the entrance of the cave. The big cave was immense and dramatic like it was supposed to be. But the weird thing was it was lit up by coloured strobe lighting. Fake spurting water fountains were dotted here and there. Nothing natural about it.

I had some questions but the guide kept well away from us. Ever since Mum had been so rude to him in front of everyone, he had avoided her, Tyrone and me and, for some reason of his own, Mrs Harris and Zoe who had done nothing to him at all. Now, after this recent showdown, he also ignored the professor. This left only Sanjay and his family. He was showing them a crumpled bank note; I knew what it was. It was one with a picture of one of the islands in the harbour on it. They were looking back at him, politely but in a mystified way. I kicked at a bit of precious thousands of years old limestone on the way out and didn't care.

That evening, as we waited for our meals to be served the professor, who was at another table, clicked his fingers and ordered a bottle of red wine. Mum also ordered one, poured a glass for herself and waved the bottle at Mrs Harris who batted it away with her hand.

In between courses, the professor and his girlfriend smooched again. When he clenched his great pig paw onto her arm, she didn't even flinch. Either she liked being pawed or she had gotten used to it. I turned back to our table. Mum poured another glass. Zoe watched the professor and his girl. Scornfully. I raised my eyebrows at her to show I agreed with her. She acted like she didn't see me.

Tyrone chose that moment to launch into one of his long diatribes which no one ever understands, take it from me. 'Epic fail,' he said, eventually, and stopped.

'Epic fail,' repeated Sanjay's wife who had been listening politely. 'What a fascinating phrase.' The daughter rolled her eyes at her brother and they both sniggered. I could see the boy mouth the word, 'Fail.'

When we were kids Mum used to tell people if they asked that there was nothing wrong with Tyrone, he just marched to the music of a distant drum. I never got it. I had to walk to school with Tyrone and he walked just the same pace as me.

Mum waved the bottle again at Mrs Harris who smiled without showing her teeth and shook her head.

After dinner, the guide came around and handed out trip evaluation sheets for each table to fill in. Mum grabbed the sheet before Mrs Harris could even reach for it. She started filling it in, ticking all the boxes beneath the heading on one end that said 'Poor.' She began writing furiously in the space for comments before moving across to sit with Sanjay's family. 'How long are you in Vietnam?' I heard her ask. The waiter came round to get people to sign the chit for the dinner and the drinks, and Mrs Harris said in a clear firm voice, 'We will have two separate bills, please.' Nice one, Mrs Harris.

I went outside onto the gangway. We had arrived in a small bay – in the China Sea, the guide told us, where we would now rest up for the night, away from the storm. I remembered he'd said about it being foreign waters. Zoe came outside and lit up a cigarette. I could just see her silhouette.

'Some trip,' I said. 'F-f-freezing.'

It was an idiotic thing to say.

Zoe drew in on her cigarette.

I leaned against the deck. The wooden plank along the top wobbled. Loose on one end. Pretty crappy and weathered from years at sea, I guessed.

'T-thought it was supposed to be h-hot in Vietnam,' I added, by way of explanation. I could hear myself stammering again. The ice-cold wind wasn't helping. I knew I must've sounded like some dumb kid who didn't know anything. Except it was true. What with Mum booking this trip in a big hurry.

I heard Zoe sigh. A waft of cigarette smoke came towards me. 'That's Ho Chi Minh City in the south,' she said. 'Not all of Vietnam.'

The boat gave a sudden strange lurch and knocked me towards the edge of the deck. I retched and felt my eyes water. When I looked up, Zoe had stubbed out her cigarette, leaving the butt on the deck, and gone inside.

I went back. There was only Mum, the professor and the Brazilian woman in the room. They were sharing a table.

The professor waved the bottle of red towards Mum. She nodded.

I felt sick, I wasn't sure why. Maybe because somehow I just knew what this would lead to. She'd launch into her story. Soon they'd hear how she gave up her chances of being a scientist at a big laboratory in Sydney when she married my dad and went to work on the farm with him. How his parents had put the farm in a family trust years before, which then meant he could rip her off in the divorce settlement and get away with it; and now he was marrying some young tart, young enough to be his daughter. Right about now, as it happened while we were here in Vietnam.

I left them to it. There was nothing I could do to stem the flood. I stood on the side deck for a while watching the neighbouring boats, all moored in the same bay as ours. There was one not far from us, also moored in the darkness. I could see the lights on its walkway. Back in the cabin, Tyrone was sitting upright on his bed, on top of the cover. Guarding something or warding off something or other unseen by me, I guessed. I left the heat pump on but turned off the light and got into bed. A little later, I heard footsteps. When I pulled the curtain back, the professor's girlfriend was passing by, on the way to their cabin.

I woke up to noises along the corridor. I recognised Mum's high-pitched voice. The one she got when she was excited or angry. When I opened the door, no one was there. I turned the light on. Tyrone was sitting on the edge of his bunk, staring past me, his long dark eyelashes fluttering. I went outside and followed the sounds a little further down the boat towards the front.

It was dark but the side lighting illuminated the two figures standing by the edge of the deck: Mum and the professor. They hadn't seen me or heard. The professor reached out and pulled my mother to him. It seemed a while before Mum struggled free. She shoved him backwards, wiped her mouth with her hand and spat on the ground.

'Bastard. What in hell-?'

The professor cut her off. 'You were asking for it, you stupid bitch.' He didn't shout. Just said it nastily. 'No wonder your old man took off. Amazed he lasted so long.' He went to push her away. I stepped towards him just as Mum whacked him on the shoulder. Hard enough for him to lurch against the side of the boat.

'Christ.' A harsh intake of breath. He struck her across the right side of her face. He stood there, swaying.

'You s-s-shit.' I was right in front of him now. I kicked him in the thigh almost at the same time as Mum struck him again. He was a big solid man and could easily have knocked either of us out, singly.

Now though, his body wavered, leaning backwards. Then the boat gave a huge lurch again, our side of the junk listing downwards towards the water. He spun fully, all of him, flat onto the deck beside us. He hit the deck with a heavy thwack, moaned, and then went silent. 'Sh – sh shit,' I said. 'Oh, shit.'

Someone bumped into me. It was Tyrone, now leaping onto the edge of the decking, flinging his cloak out, and chanting one of his incantations.

'Sh- shut up. Shut up.' The words resounded around us, echoing loudly.

He was so surprised he stopped.

An alarm sounded. A disembodied message said to go to the other end of the boat. I looked down at the professor, still lying inert. 'Quick, you go,' I said, pushing them both forwards along the front deck. Water was already crashing over the side as I followed behind. Then a door opened and Mrs Harris appeared, Zoe following her.

'The boat,' I shouted. 'It's going to sink.' There was no time to go in search of the life boats. The lights above the deck were already flickering. They'd go out completely soon. The others stared at me, as if they couldn't hear me. 'Jump over the rails.' I had to shriek now. 'Into the water. Go on, quick. Swim to the other boat.'

'Wha – wha-?' Mum clutched the boat railing. 'Ty?'

'Go.' I helped her climb over, gave her a push, heard her splash into the water. Mum was a strong swimmer. Had always been. From beneath, she shouted to Tyrone to jump in. To my surprise, he did as he was told. Zoe had taken a lifebuoy from the wall on the deck and was helping her mother whose fingers were so chilled she had been unable to put it on. But then the boat heaved again, sickeningly. I watched Mrs Harris jump, before I grabbed Zoe, pulling her with me. We landed in the freezing water, still together. Then moments later the crew from the boat also leapt into the water, shouting, floundering, and threshing about in the sea. Some began doing weird doggy paddle strokes and trying to keep afloat.

The water in Halong Bay was colder than the pool I'd learned in, the sea choppier, and my legs felt numb. I panicked and flailed for a moment.

Then I heard it. A distant voice that I dimly recognised, from far away, someone beside me urging me on, telling me it wasn't a lot different from being in the swimming pool. 'Swim to the other boat,' I told Zoe and we both began to swim. When I looked back, our boat had changed direction. It went upright. And then it was gone, all of it, the entire two decks, down, deep into the water. A hollow black gap filled the space where there had been light.

People from the other boat called out instructions, shouting us on, and reaching out to grab us. And then we were beside it and I felt myself pulled, heavy and panting, onto the deck.

'Jake,' I heard a voice say. Mine.

Someone had put a blanket around me. Zoe lay beside me, also under a blanket. My fingers were so cold it took me a minute to realise we were holding hands. Around us I could hear vomiting and weak cries from the Vietnamese crew. I looked about for Mum and saw her further along the deck, her arms around Tyrone. A guide from the boat we were now on came up to me, holding a notebook, wanting to write down our names.

The Brazilian woman was lying under another grey blanket.

There was no sign of Sanjay and his family. Their rooms had been on the other side of the boat. I thought about the heat pumps in each of the cabins, how they made you feel sleepy with so much warmth in an enclosed space.

Our guide came up to Mum and crouched down.

'I manage to wake the lady,' he said, indicating the Brazilian woman. 'She came out from the cabin. But not the man.' He was crying. 'I didn't see him anywhere. No time to look for him.'

I sat up and pulled the blanket closer around me. 'Are you okay, Mum?' I asked.

Mum looked like she was out of it still. 'Wha – wha happened?'

'Accident.' It was the captain, standing beside the guide. 'Boat goes to one side. Splash.' He glanced at me. 'Lucky you were awake.' He wasn't going to say anything further.

He moved away from us, down the deck. Someone called out the harbour police were on their way. They would want to know what happened.

It's been six months since that night. Mum and I have never talked about what happened. Sometimes I think she has no memory of it. Other times I see her giving me an odd look. She's no longer drinking and she sees a counsellor. I think that, finally, she's talking to someone about Dad letting Jake have a go on the farm bike and the accident that killed him. But what do I know? I've even tried asking Zoe at school about it all, what she thinks. She's said to be patient.

Tyrone still thinks he has powers, but now he's stopped saying Epic Fail, so that's one good thing. It reminded me too much of Sanjay and his family. I still think about them. I can't help myself. I see the water coming into the cabin and filling it, and the two kids maybe waking, thinking they're still dreaming. I liked those kids. Oh, and I worked out why I hated the professor so much for slobbering over his young girl-friend like he did. But there's no one I can tell. Not even Zoe.

THE SECRETS WITHIN HARTWICK MANOR

BY LAUREN WORDSWORTH

OLD MONEY GONE TO WASTE, THAT'S WHAT THEY CALLED IT; THE last 400 years eroded into derelict ruin. The Hartwick's last remaining heir had 'run-off' with a local girl decades past. His mother, Mrs Katherine Penelope Hartwick, had withdrawn entirely from society as a consequence of her son's actions and the enduring great depression she suffered. The handful of staff employed at Hartwick Hall over time similarly vanished into thin air, with various excuses provided for their absence over the years. The locals, however, refused to believe the stuttered words of old Billy Jones, the groundskeeper. Although it was true that he was no public speaker, often it wasn't the words he spoke without authority but his eyes that gave away the fact that sinful things occurred at Hartwick Hall. This was something he could neither divulge nor explain. So, when old Billy Jones disappeared too, many thought it was good riddance to bad news. As far as they were concerned, Hartwick Hall was cursed, no matter how grand it appeared.

The dilapidated hall stood stoically, surrounded by a protective fortress of overgrown trees, hedges and rusted wrought-iron gates. Brambles had sprouted like a plague, stretching and spreading through the cracks of the gravelled paths, flowerbeds and the driveway, consuming all vibrant life, covering them in a thick nest of thorns. They reached out like gnarled fingers, ready to snatch at anything that moved within reach, viciously wounding those careless enough to get too close. The fountain centre stage of the garden no longer pumped water out gracefully. Instead, it relied purely on nature's mercy, with the stagnated water dripping slowly from the crumbling bottom.

The gates were covered with various brambles and weeds, which were tangled and entwined with each other, adding further reinforcement should anyone wish to gain entry. There was enough to view through the narrow slits yet to be filled. He stepped back to admire the worn-out property and whistled softly. An excitement flowed within his veins whenever he saw an abandoned building, but this one, this one was different. This one was personal to him alone, his birthright, by all accounts. His warm brown eyes twinkled with delight and wonder. They were just about visible under the unruly mop of raven hair.

He slung the rucksack he'd brought to the ground and took out his knife. Soon enough, the slight sound of snipping brambles rang sweetly in his ears. He worked quickly, ignoring the thorns continually piercing his skin. Instead, he focused on breaking the entanglements stretching around the edges of each gate, pulling them away roughly before tossing them to the side in a pile.

His thick fingers curled around the railing of the gate, the odd bramble still stabbing him with a vengeance. "Shit." He murmured, pulling a thorn from his thumb.

He pushed his full weight against the gates. His boots slipped on the loose gravel, the gates creating a last resistance. At last, the rust within the hinges gave way, and with a determined shove, the gate let out a high-pitch metallic screech that reverberated within the grounds.

He picked up his rucksack, slinging it over his muscular shoulders, and wandered slowly into the gardens. He stuck to the driveway, its outline just about visible. Sand coloured gravel refused to crunch under his footsteps, the many weeds providing a soundproof barrier as he took in what were once grand surroundings. The silence was welcoming, and he made his way to the front of the manor.

The front door was weathered but solid. Its wood, discoloured from the continual bashing of nature, desperately needed attention. It seemed surprising that the door remained on its hinges. The large handles were no longer shiny, covered by layers of dirt, grime, and dust. He placed his hand on one of them and pushed gently, and it opened with a slow, low creak. The setting sun cast little light into the large entrance. He wondered for the briefest of moments whether or not to introduce himself, although he doubted he would receive a reply.

He planted his rucksack on the worn and dirty floor again, putting the knife back into the bag. Instead, he took out two torches. He switched the first one on, shining it into the dark hall to ensure it worked. The other, which was attached to a fabric band, he slipped onto his head. He swung the bag back onto his shoulder and strode inside, flashing his torch slowly around the walls.

His boots thudded gently on the wooden floor. The once elegant, patterned wallpaper had faded and peeled away from the walls, hanging limply. Loose plaster from the ceiling had scattered like debris on the floorboards, crunching faintly under his feet. Yet, the floor itself seemed unphased by the neglect. The hall held two curved decaying staircases leading to the upper floor. The bannisters were cracked and broken in various places, each spindle connecting one thick cobweb to the other. He traced his fingers over a standing newel post, appreciating the craftsmanship.

A short rattling sound echoed from deep within the manor. He jumped defensively before shaking his head, a soft laugh escaping his lips, It's an empty building, Phillip. Just like the hundreds of others you've been in.

He quickly looked in each of the rooms on the ground floor. Most of the doors had warped with dampness. Some refused to fit within their frames. The high ceilings were marked with various damp patches. Every sofa smelt musty. A thick layer of dust coated each arm, enhancing the threadbare edges. The rugs showed clear signs of being moth eaten. He opened the many different drawers, which revealed nothing of real value, not that he'd take it. He was there to be a witness.

Upon entering the dining room when he heard a large thud directly above him. The windows rattled responsively, and he backed quickly out of the room, focusing the torch beam on the ceiling above. He thought he was perhaps being signalled to leave, but as he got to the hallway, shuffling footsteps suddenly changed his mind. He made his way up the stairs, one tentative step after another, most of the stairs sagging tiredly under his weight.

The carpet was incredibly dusty, yet the trail was clear. The dust had been disturbed; surprised, he looked around hesitantly, "Hello?"

His greeting received no response. He made his way along the corridor. An old switch caught his attention, and he flicked it down. The lights initially flickered for a few moments before illuminating the wide hallway. It amazed him that the old electrics still worked. Long dust webs hung from the ceiling and the glass lampshades. He'd almost forgotten why he was up there when wheezing coughs caught his attention.

Touching the polished handle, he opened the door slowly, immediately coming face to face with the weary Mrs Hartwick resting in her chair, a long wooden vine-like cane propped beside her. He stared at her in disbelief. "I'm sorry, I thought... I thought the building was abandoned," he rambled with guilt and shame.

She looked at him, then turned her attention to the world outside. She took deep breaths before speaking, her voice soft and tired, each sentence a visible strain on her body. "I heard you come in via the gates. Are you here to loot?" she raised a wrinkled hand, beckoning him to come closer.

He shook his head. "No, Ma'am, I just wanted to see the beauty of the building and explore the forgotten, to see the place of my..." his voice trailed off, not wanting to announce his heritage to the stranger before him.

She gave a sad smile. Her emerald green dress was frayed and dirty, showing clear signs of deterioration. It hung loosely from her bony frame. She didn't meet his eyes; she seemed to wish to focus on anything but him. "I had a son once. You remind me of him," she stated ruefully, pointing at a single picture frame on her bedside table.

"Do you mind if I look at the picture?" he asked.

She nodded, staying silent. He took the picture in his hand and curiously traced a finger over the young man's face. The similarities between himself and the man were uncanny, except for the eyes. His eyes were more almond-shaped. He looked at the woman once more and cleared his throat. "He looked like a brilliant young man,"

The racking coughs escaping her body camouflaged her hoarse laugh. Phillip put down the frame and stood in front of her awkwardly for a moment. Suddenly, it felt like he'd invaded her privacy. "I'm really sorry for intruding. I'd have never-"

"I've not had a visitor in years. What is your name?" she continued. "Phillip," he replied hesitantly.

"Do you like my house, Phillip?" she asked quietly.

The question stunned him to silence. Her head snapped back in his direction, and her eyes narrowed. The wrinkles on her face deepened with her frown. Phillip nodded politely. "It is a grand house. I can only imagine how beautiful it looked decades ago."

"Decades?" she muttered. "Has it been that long?" she sighed, thoughtfully placing her hands on her creased face.

"What is your name?" Phillip asked curiously.

She looked out of the window, her voice dry and raspy. "Penelope... Hartwick,"

He'd had suspicions from the moment they met, but the confirmation still felt like a punch to the gut. An overwhelming feeling of pity for her filled him. He swallowed the lump in his throat and knelt in front of her, touching her knee kindly. "Can I do anything for you?"

She put her hand on his, her breaths coming in rasps. Phillip could see her eyes were starting to cloud over, and his sorrow for her deepened. He was no fool. Even he could see that she was trapped within her own home and left to decay with it. "I could call an ambulance and get you some help," he offered.

She shook her head. "Billy will be back soon. He went to finish the gardening."

Phillip looked down at the dusty floor, unable to bring himself to tell her that there was no one but them in the building. Her long fingers snaked around his wrists tightly. "Billy is a good man, not like my Rupert. Rupert ran off with some local harlot and the staff; they knew!" she breathed in short, rapid breaths, "When she spent all of his fortune. She left him, and Rupert came running back here..." her words trailed off, her chest rising and falling sharply.

Phillip didn't move. If she was unburdening herself, it was best that she do it now. He wasn't sure she would be alive much longer. She covered her mouth as she coughed violently. She released him, wiping some phlegm from her mouth, "He abandoned all of us... so when he came back, we didn't welcome him with open arms... I had him meet me in my sunroom instead, and Billy..." her words trailed off again.

Phillip nodded in feigned understanding. "I'll find Billy for you."

She looked back to the window, the warm sun rays cascading over her chair. Her lips pursed thoughtfully as she grasped his wrist again. "No one leaves!" she shrieked possessively.

"Let go of me," he commanded firmly.

Her face had twisted into a fit of rage. He pulled his hands free of her grip, the indents of her nails visible on his skin. He watched the rage melt away, replaced by a soft, frail face that peered out of the window again. "Are you here to torment me some more, Rupert?"

Phillip decided the only kindness he could offer her was freedom away from this place. The derelict hall was slowly becoming her tomb. To him, it was sheer amazement that she had survived here this long without assistance. "I'll be back soon," he vowed.

He returned downstairs silently, took his mobile from his pocket, and pressed 999. A soft rumbling sound, followed by a low groan, echoed from the dark corridor he'd half explored. His finger hesitated over the dial button. Something about the place gave him the creeps. He shuddered at the darkness beckoning him forward—a metal clatter from within the long hallway made every hair on his body stand on edge. For a moment, he wondered if Penelope was right about Billy and if he was tending to her needs. Maybe, in this case, it would be better to find him first. He thought before sliding his phone back into his pocket.

The rumbling sound came again, longer this time and louder. He flicked on his head torch and continued to follow the direction the noise came from. A breeze seeped through a warped window frame, moving the curtains just enough to make Phillip do a double take. He shuddered uncertainly, convinced people were lurking within the shadows.

He rushed forward, desperate for any form of natural light to stop the tricks of his imagination. The twists and turns finally. He turned a corner, coming face to face with his reflection. He caught himself before he yelped; relief filled him, and he sighed.

The door, although wooden, had a large window in the centre; it was cracked in multiple places, but he could see inside clearly enough if he pressed his face close to the glass. The sunroom was vast, holding a variety of plants he couldn't name. Some looked exotic, almost danger-ous; it seemed incredible to him that they were still alive. He noticed several panes in the glass roof had fractured - enough to let the rain in whilst keeping the worst of the elements out. The plants ranged all over the floor and up the long, narrow windows that housed them. They'd thrived untouched for years within their self-created ecosystem.

His curiosity grew at the flourishing jungle before him. He opened the door carefully to enter. It juddered in response; the hinges threatening to pull from the wooden frame. He instinctively grabbed the rest of the door to steady it. The air that hit him on release smelt surprisingly sweet and rotten. He coughed as the smell hit the back of his throat and covered his mouth as he stepped inside. The luscious reds, purples, oranges, blues, and various shades of green were a sight to behold. He closed the door gently behind him. The plants had exploded from their vases, scattering soil across the floor, thick roots stretched out into a gnarled wreathe, camouflaging the tiles below. It was then that he noticed a pair of discarded shoes. He bent down to inspect them more closely. Were it not for the erosion of the leather, he might never have seen the protruding femur from underneath the mass entanglement of roots.

He gasped, stumbling back, and his foot landed on something spherical, which shattered instantly under his weight. His hand steadied, and his torch beam highlighted the floor to reveal the broken pieces of a skull. He froze, his lungs refusing to work. He could feel his heart pound fearfully within his chest and shone the torch around the room slowly. Only then did he see the various human remains the plants had entombed. He doubled over, covering his mouth. It's a tomb! His mind frantically screamed at him. His body heaved aggressively in response to the sight before him. He tried to move, but his feet were already engulfed in the thick mud swamp, which sucked hungrily at his feet, refusing to give way to any resistance he offered.

Mrs Hartwick had left the sunroom over the various decades unattended, allowing the flowering plants room to spread and grow. Continual dampness within the air and on the plants had rapidly attacked the wooden floorboards, making weak with rot. The volume of plants eventually forced the floor to give way, and the continual subsidence had caused the room to sink deep into the mud. Had he paused and looked closely, he would have noticed the slant of the room. Now he was stuck. He could see it as clear as day.

Sheer panic rose within him, every fibre of his being screaming at him. He tried to yank his legs up, to no avail. He screamed, his calls for help inaudible. Followed by loud desperate pleas to Mrs Hartwick, hoping she would hear him. He struggled again, desperately attempting to free himself. A ping reminded him of the most obvious solution. He took his phone from his pocket with trembling hands and opened it, only to find the signal disappeared and no service was available. In a sheer moment of panic and frustration, he threw it despairingly at the windows. The plants that had grown tall and broad deflected it with ease. He tried once again to lift each leg individually, to pull them from the vines that had snaked so easily around his boots, trying to loosen them from nature's grip. The roots beneath the soil seemed to shift towards him, wrapping tighter around his ankles and legs, grasping at his wrists.

His screams and shouts continued, further exhausting him. The sun was already beginning to set. Darkness slowly began to creep towards him again. His muscles burned as he struggled to free himself. Hours later, he resigned himself to the quietness the night brought. The occasional noise had him convinced the plants were alive. He breathed steadily. His throat felt as if it had been ripped in two, irritated by the piercing screams and shouts. He remained still throughout the night, refusing to lie within the mouth of the abyss.

The sun eventually rose, signalling the start of the next day. His legs, for all their fighting in the initial hours, had only sunk deeper into the sticky mulch, which refused to release him. All of his muscles ached, exhausted from bearing his weight in a single position. His rucksack lay discarded, splattered in mud. 'Please, someone help,' he whispered hoarsely. His lips were dry, and intense pangs of hunger quickly followed the loud gurgle of his belly.

By midday, he'd cried enough on and off that his tear-stained cheeks and puffy eyes had become as sore as his throat. The overwhelming fatigue and desperation to be free churned deep within him, heightening his sense of urgency. His attempts to escape had lessened, his eyes determinedly fighting the desire to close. His body swayed with each attempt. The moment he resigned himself to his fate, his eyes shut firmly. His body, full of exhaustion, accepted its fate and fell backwards, landing softly on the cushioned, damp ground in an awkward position.

He hadn't expected or wanted to wake again, but his eyes opened to the sunlight spilling through the glass roof. His mind immediately looped back to being stuck, and he pulled his legs gently; to his shock and relief, they moved with ease; they were free. He stood up gingerly, his muscles rigid and constricted. Knowing he had to leave and escape this place. He stretched over to grab his rucksack and succeeded. He pulled out his knife, hacking at the plants covering the window next to him. His strength was waning quickly, his half-replenished energy quickly sapped from the quick movements, but he wouldn't give up; he couldn't. Eventually, the plants relented, allowing him to squeeze through the gap.

He used the knife's hilt to smash the window. The first attempt formed spiderweb cracks spreading to the edges. He used the hilt again; the glass exploding outwards. Large fragments dropped to the floor and shattered on impact; fresh air hit him immediately, the tinkling of glass sounding softer against the paved stone. He took one last look at the gap before squeezing through. An inconspicuous root caught his foot, making him stumble forward and land on all fours. He took deep, relieved breaths, ignoring the tiny shards of glass piercing his flesh.

He trudged forward, his legs shaking from the tremendous ordeal. Walking around the grounds no longer held any wonder for him. When the open gates came into view, he ran towards the exit; his legs widened in stride as he refused to remain in the damned place a moment longer. Phillip focused on his escape and didn't look back, the thoughts of saving Mrs Hartwick long forgotten.

He didn't see Mrs Hartwick standing at the window watching him intently, her soil-covered hands pressed firmly against the windowpane. Her green dress glimmered in the sunlight like a beacon. As he left the confines of her home, she banged feebly on the windows, her mouth agape, released screeching wails of, "Rupert, don't leave me!"

The last words of Mrs Hartwick echoed eerily within the halls of Hartwick Manor for years to come.

DIRTY LAUNDRY

BY AVA MING

I DON'T KNOW THE EXACT MOMENT WHEN I REALISED THE WOMAN I fancied was my boyfriend's daughter.

It could have been that first time in the laundrette when her soiled clothes rinsed away smelly grime in favour of lavender scented fabric softener. It could have been when she laughed a velvety-musical echo which settled all over me like honeyed wisps. Or, perhaps it was when she exposed her inner shyness, making me want to wrap her within my naked arms and protect her from her own fears.

I guess there was a family resemblance between Sophie and Anthony, but why would I notice? Falling for my boyfriend's progeny isn't something I make a habit of.

There was one exquisite moment when I thought we were going to be okay. We were vibing, you know? And it was new and shiny and sweeeeet! But so swiftly, things went pear-shaped and I was nobody's lover, just my own damn fool. It will never happen again, that's for sure.

Sophie sat on the unyielding, plastic grey-brown bench opposite the large washing machines, the ones able to handle a super winter-weight duvet without straining. Mrs. Mistry piped Stevie Wonder classics into the narrow laundry room to ease the boredom of watching dirty clothes plough through prescribed cycles of cottons, acrylics and coloureds. The speakers were blown, distorting the genius of Stevie's harmonica.

I'd come for my Avon catalogue but there were none on the counter so I'd dithered, unsure whether to ask Mrs. Mistry for a spare or leave it for another month. That's when Sophie caught my eye.

It was strange really. I'd occasionally seen her around but not paid her much attention, too busy, I guess. But today, with no Avon goodies to distract me, I noticed Sophie was gorgeous.

She sat with her legs uncrossed, knees apart, her hands palms down and tucked underneath her thighs. She wore snug navy jeans and a matching denim jacket over a white vest top. Her dyed dark blonde hair was set in waves moulded close to her scalp; a kind of Parisian black woman chic, and she was totally absorbed by the swish-swash of the soapy bubbles beating against the washer's glass door.

I had to discover if this woman might be okay with me loving her, so I peered into her machine pretending it was my own weekly wash.

'You've got the wrong one, that's my stuff.' Sophie came out of her reverie, pointed with a swing of her elbow, swung her legs back and forth, pragmatic about my intentional error.

'I'm always doing that!' I fake tittered, tutted and rolled my eyes. 'S'probably mine over there.' I gestured vaguely about the room.

'They're all alike, should have colour coding or something!'

The ripples of Sophie's chuckle, like the melody in her voice, sparked tiny tingles in the pit of my stomach.

'I'm Nisha.' I wriggled my fingers at her even though she was close enough for me to notice her translucent hazel eyes bordered by a darker brown rim.

'Sophie.'

'Wasn't there a black Queen Sophie once?'

'Distant relative.' She laughed. 'What's Nisha short for?'

'Tanisha. Sounds a bit naff now but it was ahead of its time back then!'

'Pain coming here init? You'd think my man'd be ashamed to see me lugging around bin liners and buy me a washer-dryer.'

'Yeah.' I didn't want to hear about her partner.

'He's got one more chance,' Sophie continued, her voice rising in expectation. 'My birthday's coming up.'

'Happy birthday in advance!' I smiled, secretly wishing she'd stop going on about her guy. All I wanted was to hold her, caress her and breathe in her smell to see what type of perfume she wore. I wanted to decipher the messages in her eyes and see if she had any for me. I thought she probably did. I hoped so. It was in the way she smiled at me so readily and the way her eyes twinkled when they met mine. More than anything I wanted to press my lips against hers, ease my tongue inside her mouth and kiss her.

'Avon! Campaign seventeen.' Mrs. Mistry signalled from the counter. I scurried over, glad to get away before Sophie felt my longing.

'Sophie, you take a book. Cosmetics, perfumes. Things for ladies like you.' She waved a catalogue at her.

'Next time.' Sophie called back, transferring her clothes from washer to dryer.

'Next time, next time? When is that?' Mrs. Mistry grumbled. 'And you take nothing from book sixteen, Nisha.' She snapped, pouring her bad mood all over me.

'All the bargains were in book fifteen.' I bristled at being scolded. 'I lose interest if it ain't buy one, get one free.'

'Young women have too much money,' Mrs. Mistry cut me off. 'In my day, the men have all the money, first your father, then your husband.'

She could talk, considering how many side hustles she had going on! I'd have probably saved myself about sixty quid a month if I wasn't an Avon junkie. Mrs M. slid me the brochure, rubbed the small of her back and swallowed two tiny white pills without any water.

'When can I get my stuff?' I hoped it would coincide with Sophie's next wash-day, whenever that was.

'Two weeks, Tuesday. Wednesday. Same, same.' Mrs. Mistry said.

'See ya, Nish.' Sophie called out as I left.

I liked how she'd doubly shortened my name from Tanisha, to Nisha, to Nish. I liked the way her jeans hugged her bottom, and I liked how her voluptuous bust accentuated her flat stomach.

'Yeah, see ya!' I replied, while my senses urged, "soon."

'What you doing month end?'

Anthony sipped his wine. He always waited until we were eating to discuss plans, as if he thought a good meal would make me more amenable. He didn't need to try so hard, having him at my table was enough.

'What's going on?' I sipped the watermelon and ginger he'd just juiced, adding a splash of vodka when I'd begged, pretty please.

'Family gathering, wanna come?' He chewed and spoke at the same time, relishing his well-done steak and picking at his vegetables. 'Surprise birthday party. My daughter's.'

'Cool. How old?'

Anthony curled his top lip and squeezed his eyes, calculating. 'Um, thirty-

one.' He pouted, bothered because his daughter was only a year older than me.

'Are we ever gonna get over this age thing or is it gonna break us apart?' I put my arms around his neck, hoping for an honest answer to my question.

'God only knows,' he said.

I suppose that was honest enough.

I'd first seen Anthony in a club up town a few months back. He'd stood at the bar watching me party with my girls, raising his glass in a small salute when we made eye contact. I clocked his good looks and full, rich brown lips. Couldn't see his body, the place was too crowded, but he was touching six-foot with long legs, perfect for a 5ft 9" black woman like me. After a couple of hours my group was looking to swerve to the next spot, I considered inviting him but by then he was already ghost. I figured he'd probably gone home to his wife.

I checked my socials on the regular but there was no sign of him lurking. A few weeks later I'd opened a copy of the local newspaper to see a feature on him in the small business section. His name was Anthony Stone and he was a chemist. I had no interest whatsoever in his profession, science bored me silly, but I lit up when I read that he was single.

A few weeks later the club had a reggae night. I went alone and dressed to kill. My bare shoulders glistening, high heeled sandals showing off my toned calves and a mini skirt wrapped so tightly around my butt it might as well have been painted on. Half an hour later, Anthony wandered in.

'Where've you been?' He leaned in close so I could hear him over the music.

'Around.' I kept it cool. 'Waiting for you to come find me.'

'Mission accomplished.' He'd whispered, sending chills down my spine. He drew me closer until our hips were touching and we whined together till the small hours of the morning.

***

'Hulloo-oo!' I rapped on the counter in the launderette with the knuckles of my free hand, my car keys and Avon brochure clutched in the other. The laundrette smelt like fresh lemons, must have been a new brand of soap powder filling the machines. Mrs. Mistry shuffled through from the back, frowning at nothing as usual.

'Your friend, Sophie, she's not here.' Mrs. Mistry checked my Avon order form to see how much commission she'd get while in the background a customer added money to a machine, a succession of coins plink-plinking into the slot.

'You clairvoyant now?' I asked her, scanning the empty benches, idly noting the worn operating instructions taped to the walls, bothered she'd guessed Sophie was on my mind.

'How long till my order arrives? I'm running out of that cream and I can't get it anywhere else.'

'Why you are looking somewhere else? You stick with me and Avon.' She opened the hatch surprising me. I'd never seen anyone else go behind the counter. Even her sons had to stand on the public side.

'Come, while the shop is quiet.' She waved me through. 'Today I read for you. Give you good advice.'

'I'm fine. Don't wanna be a bother.' I scratched the back of my head, patted my weave back into place and settled myself into the thickly padded armchair.

'You long-time customer, so no pay me today. Get up, you're in my comfy chair. Sit there.' She pointed to a three-legged wooden stool.

The doorbell chimed and I strained to see over the counter, hoping.

'It's not Sophie.' Mrs. Mistry didn't even look at the door. She threw the loose end of her sari over her shoulder and scrutinized the brown lines criss-crossing my palm.

'Who is the man whose name starts with A?'

'Dunno.' I was non-committal because I'd been evicted from the cosy lounger, but my insides zinged with shock that she'd brought up Anthony.

'You're not serious about him, he should go.'

'Hey! That's not necessarily true!' Now she had my full attention. 'I could possibly, in a few years, kinda, maybe grow to love him. Ow!'

Mrs. Mistry hushed me with a squeeze of my hand. How could such a tiny woman be so strong?

'He's ready to love, but not you.'

'I should wait for a tall dark handsome stranger? Don't get too many of those around here.' I tensed expecting another painful crush of my hand to reward my sarcasm, but I was saved by the tinkling of the doorbell. Mrs. Mistry's face was impassive but I swear she noticed the light in my eyes at Sophie's arrival.

'Enough. Next time £15.00.' Mrs. Mistry opened the hatch to let me out and disappeared into the back, ignoring Sophie.

'Someone's got their knickers in a twist.' Sophie raised her eyebrows at the departing woman as she fed her washing into a machine. 'How's things with you?' She sat on her hands again, looking delicious in a simple outfit of red jeans, white t-shirt and navy jacket fitted at the waist.

'Working on a commission, practically day and night like an idiot. I always think I've got all the time in the world until it catches up with me!'

'What do you do?'

'I'm an artist. Clay work, pottery, sculpting.'

'Wow, that's different. I can't do any of that arty type stuff. Who do you work for?'

'Self-employed. I exhibit occasionally, but private commissions are my bread and butter. You'd be surprised how many people in the posh parts of town want something unique and expensive to show off to their neighbours.'

We talked easily, making space in our conversation to transfer Sophie's clean clothes from washing machine to dryer and from dryer to bin liner. Our words spilled over themselves and into each other until it was time to go.

'Where's your washing?' Sophie asked. She looked over my shoulder to the back seat of my car next to where we stood ignoring the buzz of traffic and the first fat drops of rain.

Sophie's profile was perfect. Thick straight eyelashes, an almost European nose, firm chin, gorgeous cheekbones. Even with the finest African clay and all the time in the world I couldn't have sculpted her better.

'Didn't have any. Just came to drop off my Avon order.' I was newly miserable at the thought of parting.

Sophie put her hand on my arm. I lifted her tapered fingers to my lips to warm them, conscious my body was acting of its own accord. Count to three before you do anything else my brain warned and I got all the way to *"two Mississippi"* before her sweetly scented breath mingled with mine as we kissed.

'Now what?' She drew back a little, seeming happily surprised at herself.

'You wanna follow me in your car? Come see where I live?'

She nodded. I got into my car in a happy daze. We'd kissed in broad daylight on the street, what did she think would happen in the privacy of my home?

'I'm definitely in the wrong job.' Sophie took in my space, her mouth slightly ajar. I realised I hadn't a clue what she did for a living.

'I work part-time at the RAC call centre in town,' she offered, intuitively.

'Oh.' I couldn't comment. I'd never worked in an office and didn't know anything about call centres, apart from the never-ending, press 1 for this, press 2 for that malarky, when all you want to know is how long the wi-fi's gonna be down.

'It fits in with the kid's school hours, nursery and stuff,' she continued.

'Kids?' Again my expression belied my thoughts. It was weird being faced with the reality of her life outside of the laundrette.

'Little buggers.' she scowled. 'Just joking. They're my world. Boy and two girls. Six, four, and three years old'

'Nice.' I had nothing to add to that. Couldn't see myself having kids, ever.

'You got any? Guess not, with all this white furniture and white walls. Looks good, though.' Sophie peered into the living room through the American style arch.

'Smells like flowers,' she mumbled, side-stepping into my kitchen before crossing the hall into my study. She tilted her head checking out my books. 'Ain't read nothing in ages. Not much time or energy for that with three kids. You got a garden?'

'Out there.' I pointed through the window to a small statue of a child at play, my own vanity project. I really needed to add a clay dog or something. The little sprog looked pitifully lonely.

'Nice lawn. My husband's gonna get some turf for ours, probably put up some swings for the kids. Dunno when though. He says I should stop nagging 'cos it's on his to-do list.'

I came up behind her, kissed the nape of her neck and rested my head on her shoulder, my arm loosely around her waist. I wanted her to forget about the house, her kids and her man and focus on us.

'You been thinking 'bout me?' I murmured, my lips on her earlobe.

'Yeah, kinda.' She admitted.

'Do you have other girlfriends?' I asked.

'Nope. Never.' She turned around to face me, studying me through silky lashes, half-moon dimples at the corners of her mouth, then she kissed me, longer and deeper than before.

I led her upstairs to my bedroom and drew the cream voile curtains shutting out the bleakness of the afternoon.

'You feeling me?' I checked in while easing her jacket over her shoulders and arms. She unbuttoned my blouse. I pulled gently at the straps of her bra, skimming her satin skin with a feather touch. She took my fingertips into her mouth one after the other, until a penetrating heat rose from my belly to my chest.

We lay naked on our sides, face to face, our fingers entwined. I traced the outline of her shoulders, her breasts, her stomach and her upper thighs and she mirrored my actions. I cupped the back of her head, pulled her lips towards mine. She yielded with a tiny sigh.

When I parted her legs and bowed low to inhale her scent she threaded her fingers through my hair, eyes closed, lips barely open, the tip of her tongue poking through them.

'Is it good, baby?' I took her silence as assent and continued my exploration. 'Am I moving too fast? We can go slow if you prefer. I planted tantalising kisses and offered gentle caresses as if she was my first and most important beauty.

It was a few minutes before I clicked Sophie's rhythms were no longer in tandem with mine and passion had nothing to do with the way she was gripping my hair. Her fists were clenched, her jaw was tight and her mute anger clogged the air between us. She was actively trying to hurt me!

'You...you changed your mind?' I stuttered, uncertainty ripping into my earlier confidence.

She stared rigidly at a vintage beaded glass frame on the nightstand behind me.

'S'okay, we don't have to, you know, do anything, if you don't really want to.' I sat up, covering our bodies with the bedsheet, wishing I'd had the sense to hide the picture of me and Anthony all loved up.

She shifted into an upright position, dragging the sheet taut around herself leaving me bare.

'Babe, what's the matter?' I laid a delicate hand on her, horrified when she flinched.

'Who is that? Your boyfriend?' She grimaced.

'He's not important. Just say the word, he's gone.' I snapped my fingers. 'It's not like we're serious or anything. That's just us messing about on a day out, last week, or maybe the week before I think it was...'

'-you know nothing about me, doesn't that bother you?' She cut me off from my rambling.

'I want to get to know you. I thought that's what we were doing!'

She stumbled into her underwear, interrupting herself long enough to grab the picture and thrust it at me, almost stubbing it against my nose.

'What the hell?' I scuttled sideways, tumbling off the bed onto the floor and edging back against the wall, away from her rage. My crumpled clothes twisted into knots as I struggled and failed to get dressed.

Sophie clutched the picture, mad enough it seemed, to fling it at me.

'This is Anthony Stone, right?' Her words pulsed stubbornly through gritted teeth

'Yeah, so?' Did she see the news article too? She couldn't have, she said she didn't have time to read. Tears burnt the back of my eyes and my chest hurt. Our lovemaking was over before it had properly begun and I had no clue why.

'Stone was my maiden name! This,' she shook the frame so hard it rattled, 'is my dad!'

'What!' I stared at it as if the proof was etched there in official lettering and sealed with a government stamp. 'You're joking? You gotta be!' I gulped away the scratchiness on the inside of my throat while my heart pulsed in a peculiar kind of slow-motion.

Sophie hurled the picture onto the wooden floor centimetres away from me, cracking the frame. Minute shards of shattered glass bounced against my skin, it was like being jabbed with hundreds of tiny needles.

'First the dad, then the daughter! Who's next in the family?'

'It's your birthday party soon, right?' I held up my trembling hand to calm her. 'Anthony wants to introduce me to all of you.' I flapped both hands around like an idiot, drowning in my own inadequacy. 'We were looking on Amazon for something nice, a present, I mean. I'm a bit younger than you, you see, but he said he thought he'd be okay with that, eventually. He wanted us to get on. To be friends.' I put my fingertips to my forehead and bit my lip, swimming in a sea of confusion.

Sophie zipped up her jeans and threw on her t-shirt and jacket. She put her index finger to her temple and twisted it, 'are you loco, bitch?' She snatched up her bag avoiding contact with me as if I was something slimy she didn't want stuck to the bottom of her shoe. She ran down the stairs and slammed my front door, cementing her departure.

I slithered into a corner small in my nakedness. I tucked my knees under my chin, wrapped my arms around them and succumbed to a flow of pitiful tears. The most beautiful woman I'd seen in a long time had been wrenched from my embrace by an unlikely co-incidence and there was nothing I could do but accept the stark and devastating reality that I'd lost her for good.

GIVING DEATH THE SLIP

BY KATHRYN T

MARTHA WALKED INTO THE MAKESHIFT HOSPITAL WITH determination on her face and a clipboard in her arms. Despite the somewhat earthy smell that came with living underground (and that was the only way to live now that the surface was a disease-ridden waste-land), she relaxed slightly as she strode past the long line of people in need of medical attention and into the sanctuary of the staff-only lockers area. This was somewhere where the world made sense. She was just pulling on her long white lab coat, clipboard tucked between her knees, when someone tapped her cheerfully on the shoulder.

"Martha! I was thinking you'd never arrive."

Martha shook her head fondly as she turned around. "Mickey, it's exactly the same time I always arrive. You're the one who's early. What did you forget this time?"

Despite the good natured ribbing, the two were good friends, and when Mickey looked dejectedly at his feet, Martha sighed. "What do you want, Mick?"

"I- my keys," said Mickey miserably, gesturing to the empty loop on his jacket. "They're at home."

Martha shook her head in mock disapproval. Mickey was always forgetting something, but keys were important; pass cards were all very well and good, but it was always easier just to use keys, as the electricity supply was unreliable and it was important to save it for more important things.

"I'm working with Dr Holloway today, so she can let me through. You can borrow mine. But if you forget your keys again, I'll tape them to your forehead."

Mickey chuckled at the image. "Martha, you're a godsend. No idea what I'd do without you." He picked up the chunky ring of keys in question and attached them to a clip before walking off, whistling.

Martha watched him walk away, distracted for a moment, and then picked up her pager, grabbed her clipboard and headed off to find Dr Holloway.

Several hours later, now relieved of her clipboard and with her pager clipped to her belt next to the empty keyring, Martha was just considering how best to use the thirty minutes Dr Holloway had given her before she was expected to be back on shift when her pager beeped insistently. *You are needed in the infectious ward,* it said. No explanation, no reasoning. But Martha knew the ward in question. This wasn't just a disease ward; this was the so-called 'death' ward - the price they paid for being an upper level hospital. This was the ward where the infected went to die when they'd caught one of the many surface diseases and had just a week left to scrape out an existence. Martha didn't break her stride, just turned at the next junction, speed-walking rather than running. She was the most experienced of the junior doctors; it would be bad news to everyone if they were to see her run. But if they'd called for her help, something had gone seriously wrong, because the death ward had the most tightly controlled security, and people always went in with another medic to avoid emergencies. You could survive there for fifteen minutes maximum without getting infected, if you disinfected immediately when you got out. There could be no space for error.

The door was unlocked. That was the first sign that something had gone wrong. Martha strode in, closing the door behind her, and did a quick roll call, heart thundering in her chest.

No patients missing.

No collapsed doctor on the floor.

Nobody in distress.

It felt like good news initially, but Martha had already been in there for twelve minutes, and she was fairly certain something must have gone wrong. She was just pondering that thought when her pager buzzed again. *We got you good and proper, Little Miss High-and-Mighty. Out you come, and face the consequences of an unapproved trip into the death ward.*

So it had been a joke. A sick, cruel joke. Martha turned, wondering who disliked her enough to trick her into the death ward, and froze, hand on the door handle. The door handle that she had shut behind her out of instinct when she'd come in. The door handle that needed a set of keys to open. Tension ratcheted up her spine, and Martha dropped her head to hide the sudden prick of tears in her eyes. She didn't want the infected to see a doctor cry; they had life hard enough already. Swallowing hard, she took her hand off the door and slipped into the adjoining room, closing the door behind her with a soft click and leaning against it, feet slipping against the floor so that she ended up sitting on the ground, knees pressed up to her chest, fighting back tears. She fumbled with her pager, trying to send a message out to someone - anyone - who could rescue her, but the signal cut out, leaving her stranded, every panicked breath another reminder that she would never be allowed out again, that she had just one week left to live.

It was two hours before they found her on the intermittent CCTV, curled up in that little room, practically catatonic with despair. They didn't even come to collect her, choosing to just deliver a set of keys to the room she was in via the suspiciously old-fashioned system of pipes that traversed the hospital. No human contact, no comfort, just a set of keys and a note with a specific disinfecting shower and an isolation ward on it. Martha tore up the sheet of paper, suddenly furious with her own petty mistakes, and channelled her anger into uncurling herself, holding her head high, and leaving the death ward alive for the last time.

The days passed, one tick of the clock at a time. Not even Mickey was permitted in to see Martha - just an unnamed doctor, always in a full mask, never staying for more than fifteen minutes, just long enough to collect results for tests Martha herself had carried out numerous times in practice. She knew every detail of this procedure - every thought process and chemical reaction. She'd studied them enough times. She'd never thought about what it was like from the other side of the mask; how terrifyingly isolating it could be, how much her future weighed on her mind, how every random sneeze suddenly felt like a death sentence. The countdown was like a scar across her brain. One week left to live. Three days left to live. One day left to live.

She should have died three days ago.

Two weeks after she had been infected, Martha was sitting on her bed running through the second chapter of her medical textbook in an attempt to keep herself mentally agile, the isolation and lack of stimulation almost physically painful. Her concentration was deep enough that the soft clunk of the vacuum pipe startled her, and it took her a moment to remember why the room was so deathly quiet, the subsequent ping of the slightly decrepit dumbwaiter like a gunshot into the silence. Martha stood up quickly, reading first the short message that had arrived via the pipes, then collecting the uniform that was packed into the dumbwaiter with her heart pounding. She was being released. With almost surgical precision, Martha stripped and pulled on the black combat clothes she had been given, quietly appreciating their well-tailored fit after weeks spent in the one-size-fits-nobody hospital wear. She was being released. There was a set of keys in with the clothes, and Martha clasped them hard enough to leave an imprint in her hand, the cold metal a welcome shock. Pulling herself up to her full height, Martha strode out of the door, enjoying the simple freedoms that came with a universal key, unable to believe what was happening. She was alive; more than that, she was immune, and that meant that she was free to live the rest of her life without restriction.

Two years later, Martha had discovered that the world wasn't quite her oyster yet. Aside from her ever more strenuous activities as a full time doctor in the infectious ward, there was now the increasing expectation that she would sacrifice all of her time, not only for the intensive medical tests they were running on her to try and produce vaccines, but also for the brutal moments that came with her so-called freedom. She stole through the streets alone, checking constantly that there was nobody around to see her, combat gear silent and camouflaged within the drifting smog; a wraith among a dead city. Hidden in the shadows, she watched people flit through the acrid smoke, darting between the entrances to separate underground systems like the one she had spent much of her adult life in. They didn't notice her, on her way to yet another assignment, and she supposed that was for the best. An assignment; she recoiled instinctively at the term. It was the neat, humane way that her bosses, tucked away in safety, liked to put it. Realistically, it was culling - killing animals that could carry surface diseases before they could kill you. Martha watched people donning their scuba-like masks, hurrying away out of the choking smog, and her hand went unconsciously to the brand on her collarbone which marked her out as being different from them. Though it was invisible below her layers of combat gear, it was always present in her mind, like an itch she was unable to scratch. She'd screamed when they branded her - screamed like a banshee and fought like a tiger, desperate and with nothing to lose - but it hadn't stopped the unrelenting fall of the stamp towards her flesh, burning in a symbol that would never heal. It was inhumane, she had argued later - labelling people in such an undeniable way was never the mark of a healthy society. But so much of this job was inhumane, and sometimes Martha wondered if the fight was worth it.

Eventually she reached her designated target (and how those words stung, as if it were a terrorist base, and not the last retreat of a frightened animal). Even after a year of traversing the streets alone, it was strange to see a children's playground, abandoned and destroyed beyond belief, and Martha sighed; a sigh with the weight of the world on its shoulders. There was no sign of the panic that had occurred when everyone first moved underground beyond a single child's shoe, left abandoned at the bottom of a pile of crumpled plastic that might have once been a slide, burnt beyond recognition. Pausing for a moment, Martha heard a rustle, and a squeak, and knew that whoever had called this in had, at least, got the place right. She'd always wondered where those calls came from, but she shook the thought from her mind and slipped off her restrictive stab vest, then her heavy, distinctive coat, leaving her in a black top and leggings that were more suited to the narrow, constrictive space she was about to enter. Far from being foolhardy, she felt it would be a better approach; most animals would be threatened by the armour, and she hadn't yet met an animal in this ruined wasteland she'd felt threatened by.

Crouching down, she crawled under the platform towards the source of the noise, stopping dead when she saw it. The tiny tabby grey kitten was wet through, and Martha could see each one of its bony ribs through its thin fur coat, eyes dull with cold and fear. Martha held out a hand, and it shrank back further, fur puffing up slightly in an effort to disguise its utter terror.

"It's okay," murmured Martha, crawling into the back of the hidey-hole and scooping up the kitten, knowing there was no way she could end its life, wondering how, exactly, she was going to sneak it back into her meagre apartment and nurse it back to health. And in that moment, surrounded by human-caused death and destruction, Martha wondered which one of them was truly the animal, and which one truly needed protecting.

AFTERWORD

Thank you for reading our Perfectly Formed anthology collection of short stories, written by these fantastic writers. We hope you have enjoyed what you have read as much as we did.

Junoberry Books continues to be committed to encouraging creative writing, and we will be running a number of further competitions over the course of 2024.

If you would like to enter, or you would like to stay updated with future publications, opportunities and competitions, then head to our website: www.junoberrybooks.com/short-stories

ALSO BY JUNOBERRY BOOKS

If you enjoyed reading the short stories in this collection, then you may also be interested in the following publications from *Junoberry Books* that are available in print and eBook:

CLASSIC SHORTS

We also have a range of classic short stories available, with writing from some of the best authors to have ever put pen to paper, including:

- Mark Twain
- Sir Arthur Conan Doyle
- James Joyce
- Virginia Woolf
- F. Scott Fitzgerald
- H.G. Wells
- Robert Louis Stevenson
- Kate Chopin
- Oscar Wilde
- Ernest Hemingway
- Joseph Conrad
- Philip K. Dick
- Louisa May Alcott
- Edgar Allan Poe.

The collections we have are:

- Shorts: Volume One: A Dozen Classic Short Stories

-Shorts: Volume Two: Another Dozen Classic Short Stories

-Shorts: Volume Three: Another Dozen Classic Short Stories

- Shorts: Volumes I - III: A bumper collection of 36 short stories combining all three volumes of Shorts

- Advent Shorts: Classic Short Stories for every day of Advent (An Alternative Advent Calendar)

- Twelve Shorts of Christmas: Classic Short Stories for the Holiday Season

- Another Twelve Shorts of Christmas: More Classic Short Stories for the Holiday Season

- Scary Shorts: 13 Classic Horror Short Stories

Classic Shorts

SEASONAL SHORTS: CHRISTMAS 2023

We also ran our first junior writing completion, *Seasonal Shorts: Christmas*, where young writers, aged 6 to 18, created Christmas themed short stories. We were lucky enough to have hundreds of entries into the competition, and we published three books containing the best entrants.

Our main book contained the winners and runners-up for each age category, as well as the stories that were shortlisted. It contains 24 excellent short stories covering a range of topics and ages.

We also published the stories that made our Long List in two volumes, each containing over 25 stories, with the stories included narrowly missing out making on the final cut.

Volume I contains stories from writers aged 6 to 10.

Volume II contains stories by writers who are aged 11 to 14.

ACTOR'S EDITIONS

We have also our range of Shakespeare texts that are designed to support actors, especially young actors, with their work.

Actor's Editions are specifically designed and written with actors in mind. The text is the same, with no edits or alterations. The additional elements included and the presentation makes this version what you need as an actor approaching the play.

- A no-nonsense approach to the text

- Background information on Shakespeare and the play

- Detailed synopsis, character information, key themes

- Acting tips and hints for working with Classical Theatre

- Acting techniques and approaches

- A layout to support actors when working on the text and in rehearsals

- Ample space to make notes and draw stage directions and diagrams.

Actor's Editions

Our partner company Creative Jelly work with writers on the development of their creativity, especially in writing and acting.

They run a number of online courses, training and development in a range of areas, including: Creative Writing, Prose, Scriptwriting, and Screenwriting, as well as Acting and Audition Prep.

There are different levels to undertake, from courses to help get you started in a particular area, up to advanced courses. They also work one-to-one in these areas if this is an approach that people prefer, or if they have specific requirements.

Their tutors have industry experience, are trained to MA level in Creative Writing and are qualified teachers with full DBS checks.

Check out what they have to offer at:

www.creativejelly.co.uk/writers

Printed in Great Britain
by Amazon

37015200R00078